"Know what I think?"

No, Crystal thought, she didn't know what Nathan thought, but if he came any closer, she was going to know how he felt.

"I think you like men, me in particular," Nathan said.

"Don't let it go to your head."

Heat charged through Nathan. "Would you tell me something, Crystal?"

She took her sweet time replying. "I'll try."

"I was just wondering..." He lowered his face by degrees, his mouth a hairbreadth from hers as he whispered, "How does this make you feel?"

"If you put your money where your mouth is, cowboy, you might just find out."

Dear Reader,

Get Caught Reading. It sounds slightly scandalous, romantic and definitely exciting! I love to get lost in a book, and this month we're joining the campaign to encourage reading everywhere. Share your favorite books with your partner, your child, your friends. And be sure to get caught reading yourself!

The popular ROYALLY WED series continues with Valerie Parv's *Code Name: Prince*. King Michael is still missing—but there's a plan to rescue him! In *Quinn's Complete Seduction* Sandra Steffen returns to BACHELOR GULCH, where Crystal finally finds what she's been searching for—and more....

Chance's Joy launches Patricia Thayer's exciting new miniseries, THE TEXAS BROTHERHOOD. In the first story, Chance Randell wants to buy his lovely neighbor's land, but hadn't bargained for a wife and baby! In *McKinley's Miracle*, talented Mary Kate Holder debuts with the story of a rugged Australian rancher who meets his match.

Susan Meier is sure to please with *Marrying Money*, in which a small-town beautician makes a rich man rethink his reasons for refusing love. And Myrna Mackenzie gives us *The Billionaire Is Back*, in which a wealthy playboy fights a strong attraction to his pregnant, single cook!

Come back next month for the triumphant conclusion to ROYALLY WED and more wonderful stories by Patricia Thayer and Myrna Mackenzie. Silhouette Romance always gives you stories that will touch your emotions and carry you away....

Be sure to *Get Caught Reading!*

Mary-Theresa Hussey

Mary-Theresa Hussey
Senior Editor

Please address questions and book requests to:
Silhouette Reader Service
U.S.: 3010 Walden Ave., P.O. Box 1325, Buffalo, NY 14269
Canadian: P.O. Box 609, Fort Erie, Ont. L2A 5X3

Quinn's Complete Seduction

SANDRA STEFFEN

SILHOUETTE *Romance*

Published by Silhouette Books

America's Publisher of Contemporary Romance

For Carolyn Zane—great friend, fellow writer-wife-
mom-sister-daughter-pet lover,
all with a Christian slant and a humorous flair.
Go girl!

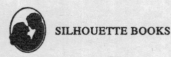 SILHOUETTE BOOKS

ISBN 0-373-19517-6

QUINN'S COMPLETE SEDUCTION

SANDRA STEFFEN

Growing up the fourth child of ten, Sandra developed a keen appreciation for laughter and argument. Sandra lives in Michigan with her husband, three of their four sons and a blue-eyed mutt who thinks her name is No-Molly-No. Sandra's book *Child of Her Dreams* won the 1994 National Readers' Choice Award. Several of her titles have appeared on national bestseller lists.

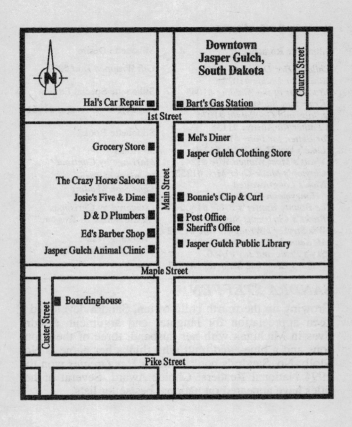

Downtown Jasper Gulch, South Dakota

Church Street

Hal's Car Repair ▄   ▄ Bart's Gas Station

1st Street

Grocery Store ▄   ▄ Mel's Diner

▄ Jasper Gulch Clothing Store

Main Street

The Crazy Horse Saloon ▄

Josie's Five & Dime ▄   ▄ Bonnie's Clip & Curl

D & D Plumbers ▄   ▄ Post Office

   ▄ Sheriff's Office

Ed's Barber Shop ▄

Jasper Gulch Animal Clinic ▄   ▄ Jasper Gulch Public Library

Maple Street

Custer Street

▄ Boardinghouse

Pike Street

Chapter One

It was spring.

Nathan Quinn wasn't quite sure how it had happened, but it had. He eased his truck past the curve where mayflowers and lady's slippers grew thick and the country road turned into a village street. Although still on the cool side, the air streaming through his open window carried the sweet scent of the first lilacs to bloom. The wildflowers had survived the long, harsh South Dakota winter. More amazingly, so had he.

He waved at the people who happened to be out in their yards, the action as natural as the way he fiddled with the worn wedding band on his finger. It was probably time he took it off, but so far he hadn't had the heart to do it. It was hard to believe his Mary had been gone more than a year. He supposed he could blame the season for putting the bounce back in his step. He sure as shootin' never intended to feel alive again at the ripe old age of thirty-eight. His body had started to awaken about the time the snow had started to melt. At first he'd done his best to ignore it. Lately he'd been thinking it would be nice to find a woman like Mary, kind and gentle and sweet. Coming to a stop at the only stop sign in the entire village of Jasper Gulch, he thought it wouldn't be easy anywhere. It would be especially difficult in a town dubbed Bachelor Gulch due to its lack of marriageable women.

Although he wouldn't say he felt lucky, he was luckier than most of the local boys. He'd had a good and solid marriage. He worked a profitable ranching operation with his brothers. And he had Holly, the best daughter in the world.

He pulled into the high school lot and parked near the spot where he'd kissed Mary the first time when they were both fifteen. He could hardly believe Holly was that age now. As far as he knew, she hadn't kissed a boy yet. Grimacing, he told himself not to think about kissing, not from a father's standpoint and not from a man's.

He glanced at his watch, strummed his fingers on the steering wheel and waited. He was early. He was always early these days. It was as if he was trying to get a head start on the rest of his life. Which was the second stupidest thing he'd ever attempted. The first, well, the first had happened a long time ago. He'd spent a lot of years beating himself up over something he couldn't change. He was a man who learned from his mistakes. There were certain things a man had control over. Not a boy, perhaps, but a man, yeah, he had control.

Punching a button, he turned on the radio, only to switch it off again less than a minute later. The tunes were too mellow these days, the lyrics too sensual for a guy who'd been without a woman as long as he'd been.

Spring had always been his favorite time of the year. He was trying to blame the way his blood was vibrating with a new sense of urgency on the season. Not that it did much good. No matter who or what he blamed, there wasn't much a man alone could do about it. Except wait for it to pass, maybe, and wonder what in Sam Hill was taking Holly so long.

A movement behind the hedge just east of the school caught his eye. It looked like one of the local men was arguing with one of the few women who had moved to town. Nathan couldn't see clearly through the sparse spring foliage, but he could make out the shape of Forest Wilkie moving stealthily closer to the only woman in town with hair that long, that blond, that wavy: Crystal Galloway.

Crystal appeared to be looking over her shoulder, her movements nervous, jerky. Forest followed her, grabbed her hair. And Nathan sprang out of the truck.

He might have expected bad behavior from Clive Hendricks or Keith Gurski, but Forest Wilkie had always been one of the good old boys. Which was what Nathan was telling himself as he sprinted across the school lawn and ducked through a gap in the hedge. There was a scuffle as he hauled Forest around to face him. Forest was shorter than Nathan, but wiry and strong. Luckily Nathan had the element of surprise on his side.

Forest gasped. "Nathan, are you crazy?"

Nathan could have asked Forest the same question, but he was saving his strength, because it was taking most of it to force Forest backward toward the building, especially with Forest resisting and that fool woman tugging on his arm and both of them talking at once.

Forest tripped, and somehow Crystal got between the two men, and the next thing Nathan knew her soft curves were pressed tight to the entire length of him from thigh to chest. Her gaze flew to his. There was softness in her moss-green eyes, and an awareness that sent his heart chugging and his thoughts scrambling. The rest of him went perfectly still.

Forest regained his footing, and Crystal turned her head and began speaking. Nathan was too aware of her scent, his body too in tune with her softness to follow what she was saying.

"...so in case there are no brave knights on white horses around to save you girls from an evil villain, otherwise known as an attacker or assailant. Let's take it from the top, shall we, Forest?"

"Whatever you say, Crys—that is, Miz Galloway," Forest answered.

Again, those moss-green eyes turned to Nathan. "Nathan?"

His gaze strayed from her eyes to her lips, which were still slightly parted after uttering his name. "Hmm?" he heard himself whisper.

"This would probably work better if you let me go now." Her voice was low and sultry, as if it was meant for his ears alone. She turned her head and called, "How about a nice round of applause for our second helper."

Her *second* helper?

Nathan was still having trouble putting two thoughts together. He couldn't get past the fact that she'd called him by name. He knew hers, of course. Everybody knew it when someone new moved to town. But the two of them hadn't been formally introduced. He didn't come into town much, and from what he'd heard, she didn't go out much.

He hadn't realized he'd wrapped his arms around her until she moved to get out of them. He liked her where she was. Right about then the high school girls watching from several feet away began to clap.

In a whoosh, it occurred to him that she'd been conducting a self-defense class and Forest was helping. The earlier scene had been staged. Nathan had gotten in the way. Was in the way still.

Outwardly he still couldn't move. Inside, his blood had thickened, was heating, pulsing. His heart chugged, and he couldn't draw a deep breath, all because of the woman tucked so nice and close to his body. Never mind that this woman wasn't petite or thin as a wisp. Like Mary had been.

Nathan came to his senses the way lightning found the

ground, with a blinding jolt followed by an ear-splitting boom. His arms fell to his sides and he took a giant backward step.

Glancing around, he was relieved to find that time hadn't stood still after all. In fact, it appeared that only a matter of seconds had passed since he'd pushed through the hedge and proceeded to make a complete fool of himself. Thankfully, the high school girls seemed to believe it was part of the act, and Forest was busy taking his place in preparation to begin the demonstration again, and didn't appear to think anything was amiss. With a wink that could easily have started Nathan's heart pounding all over again, Crystal swooped down, scooped Nathan's brown Stetson off the ground where it had landed unbeknownst to him, and handed it back to him.

Nathan cleared his throat, crammed his hat back on his head where it belonged and nodded at the girls in the audience. An instant later he backed through the hedge and ambled toward his truck where his daughter was now waiting, her violin case in tow.

Holly gave him a smile and her own special wave, one finger at a time. He returned the grin and the wave, but for once didn't hurry any too fast, putting the time it took him to stroll across the parking lot to good use.

"Hey, Daddy. You watching the demonstration?"

His answer started with a nod and ended with a shrug. On the other side of the hedge, a series of halfhearted screams rent the air, followed by Crystal calling, "Louder! You want someone to hear you, and the last thing an assailant wants is attention drawn to him."

The next series of screams were shrill enough to shatter eardrums and possibly glass.

Holly grinned again. "Isn't she the best? Jenna promised to teach me everything I'm missing."

Holly's eyes were bright, her smile more like it used to be. One of these days she would probably revert to calling him Dad again, something she'd done from the time she was eight until just before Mary had died.

He and Holly were both finding their smiles. Mary would be proud of them. Thoughts like that didn't sear a hole through him anymore. Yep, it might not hurt to start thinking about finding another woman like Mary.

By the time he climbed behind the wheel, his breathing was back to normal and his mind had done a fair job of blocking out the memory of what a chance encounter with a voluptuous blonde could do to a man's equilibrium.

It was spring.

Lo and behold, Crystal Galloway thought, it was spring. Never mind that the calendar had indicated that winter had officially ended six weeks ago. Springtime in South Dakota didn't follow the rules. It came when it was good and ready. There was something about that kind of tenacity she liked.

The last bell had rung five minutes ago, and most of the kids had left the schoolyard. A few stragglers called, "Bye, Miss Galloway!"

"Thanks for the lesson, Miss Galloway! I can hardly wait to use what I learned!"

"Remember," she replied, "self-defense isn't a game."

"We know."

Crystal caught herself staring after two girls who were rushing toward the parking lot where a yellow bus was waiting. It was something she did automatically. Sighing, she turned to Forest Wilkie. "I hope I'm not creating monsters."

Forest glanced at Crystal. "There's never been much need for that kind of self-defense around here. Still, it might come in handy to the girls who leave town for the lure of the city and better job prospects the way girls have been doing for the past thirty years."

Forest was one of several area ranchers who still held doors for women and said "yes, ma'am" and "no, thank you.'' In his thirties, he wasn't exactly what Crystal would call good-looking, but he wasn't ugly, not at all. He was average. Average build. Average height. Average intelligence. He was exactly the kind of man she would have been looking for, if she'd been looking for a man.

She knew he was lonely, just as she knew it would take but one little signal from her, be it a curl of her finger or a simple flutter of her eyelashes, and he would vie to be more than a friend. Since moving to Jasper Gulch nearly a year and a half ago, Crystal hadn't given any of the area bachelors that kind of signal. Several of them hadn't let that stop them. She'd had a dozen requests for supper and a movie those first few months. She'd even had two marriage proposals, both of which she'd flat-out turned down. And yet she'd never come face-to-face with the man who'd interrupted her demonstration a little while ago. Photographic memory aside, she wouldn't have forgotten meeting a man like him.

Forest had called the man Nathan. Judging by his build, dark hair and facial features, he was one of the Quinns. Well, well, well. Here she was thinking about him again. It had happened right after he'd ducked back through the hedge, too. To cover her own disquietude, she'd taught the girls how to scream bloody murder. Her ears were still ringing.

Forest was probably right about how much the girls here needed self-defense tactics. There wasn't a lot of crime in Jasper Gulch. Every now and then somebody would reminisce about the time one of the younger girls had stolen brownies and cookies from porches. And Crystal had been in the Crazy Horse Saloon when an infamous crook from Chicago had come to Jasper Gulch to get even with the sheriff who'd put him away. The man was behind bars for good now. And once again most people didn't even lock their doors.

According to the local men the biggest crime was how

the girls had taken to leaving town right after graduation. Some women had moved to town, and new businesses were opening, thereby giving the local girls potential jobs and reasons to stay, yet progress was slow. At last count there were still more than sixty bachelors and only a handful of marriageable women. The local boys had been in such dire straits they'd advertised for women a few years ago. Crystal had seen a follow-up article in a magazine, but she hadn't moved to this godforsaken town to find a man. She'd come because the people in the town had sounded lost and lonely. And she'd known the feeling. She had another reason, but it was a secret to everyone except her.

She took a deep breath and was almost certain she could still smell the scent of Nathan's aftershave. She tried to recall everything she'd ever seen and heard about the Quinns. Tall, dark and brooding, DoraLee Brown called them.

"What about you?" Forest asked.

Crystal scanned her memory for a hint as to what Forest was talking about. Coming up blank, she said, "What about me?"

"You fixin' to stay in Jasper Gulch?"

"Sugar," she said, smiling, "I can't imagine any other place in the world where a shriveled-up old maid like myself should be."

Forest shook his head. "If you're a shriveled-up old maid, I'm a monkey's uncle, and my only brother doesn't have any kids."

With a wink that was more than a little brash, she laughed out loud. Forest was a kind and decent man, but there were no sparks between them. Forget what the experts claimed about a woman reaching her sexual peak in her thirties. She'd assumed that, at thirty-three, she was past her prime.

There had been plenty of sparks between her and Nathan Quinn, though.

Well, well, well. She was thinking about him again. Well, well, well, indeed. She wondered how old he was and where he lived and which family of Quinns he belonged to. She could have asked Forest, but that would seem as though she were interested. And she wasn't. Interested, that is. What she was, was curious. That was all. Curious, because for the span of one heartbeat, she'd sensed that Nathan's aura had connected with hers.

Crystal was still thinking about auras when she locked the back door of the Jasper Gulch Medical Center where she spent her mornings working as a receptionist for Dr. Kincaid and her afternoons counseling patients of her own in one of the back rooms. She'd once written a thesis on Kirlian photography, also known as the art of photographing auras. She'd been fascinated by its potential use in diagnosing diseases and detecting mental and physical illness. She'd interned in that field, but it had meant spending most of her time hidden away in a laboratory. And while she had a penchant for gadgets, and laboratories had plenty of those, she wanted to be surrounded by people and natural light and old things. Most especially, she wanted to be somewhere, anywhere, where she could be found, on the off chance that—

"Harrumph!"

At first Crystal ignored the sound. She knew who'd made it. Only one person in town could whisper loud enough to penetrate steel. She hadn't taken more than three steps toward the boarding house when it came again.

Living down the block from the place where she worked had its advantages. The fact that Harriet Andrews lived on the same block wasn't one of them. Crystal smiled at Harriet, even though she knew her smile would be neither welcomed nor returned. Sure enough, Harriet raised her fleshy chin and spun around, giving Crystal the cold shoulder.

Built like a tank, Harriet was one of the nastiest gossips

in town. She spent a great deal of her day peeking through
her curtains at the people who traipsed in and out of Doc
Kincaid's office. It was generally said that the rest of Jasper
Gulch knew when a person was sick before that person did.
Harriet had been thrilled when rumors had circulated that
her only son's marriage was on the rocks, because she'd
been sure she was about to get her boy back. No one had
been more surprised than his mother when Grover, a forty-
year-old mama's boy if there ever was one, and his es-
tranged, Southern-belle wife, Pamela Sue, had come to
Crystal for marriage counseling. Grover and Pamela Sue
were working things out, and Harriet was holding Crystal
personally responsible.

Crystal took Harriet's censure in stride. Actually, she
thought it was rather laughable, but the gossip Harriet
spread about the people Crystal was trying to help wasn't
funny. She really needed to find a more private place to see
her clients. After sharing a meal with her dear friends, Brittany and Nick Colter and their two daughters, Crystal set
out to find such a place. With a map of the area in one
hand and the real estate section of the county newspaper
on the passenger seat, she drove down one dusty country
road after another.

It came as no surprise that real estate in and around Jasper Gulch wasn't exactly booming. The old Grange Hall
was for sale. It had a certain charm, but mercy, it would
take all her savings to bring it up to code.

She was on her way to the only other house listed in the
newspaper when she saw one that wasn't advertised. It sat
all by itself on a grassy little knoll, surrounded by fruit trees
and overgrown bushes. It was...charming, so charming in
fact that she swore the house winked at her. It was probably
an optical illusion created by the angle of the setting sun
glinting off the upstairs windows. She stopped at the end
of the driveway and stared at the unusual structure with its

wraparound porches and overgrown yard surrounded by a thorn-covered stone fence.

She'd traveled abroad years ago, visiting ancient castles and mystical ruins, natural wonders and disappearing rain forests. They were all lovely, amazing, really. But this, now this one was unlike anything she'd ever seen. Small and square, it had three stories, ornate trim and a stained-glass window in the front door. It was unusual, eccentric, even. She loved it immediately and wondered whom the house belonged to.

On a whim she parked her car beneath the shade of a gnarled old apple tree about to blossom and strolled all the way around the outside of the house. A woman had lived here. Judging by the color of the house, she'd probably lived here alone. Crystal simply couldn't imagine any of the local ranchers or cowboys agreeing to live in anything painted that particular shade of pink.

She didn't know what possessed her to hurry up the steps and tiptoe across the porch. She glanced over her shoulder, then peered through the window. Sheets covered the furniture, which lent further credibility to her theory that nobody lived there. On a lark, she reached for the screen door. It opened on squeaky hinges. The inner door was unlocked, too. Promising the house she wouldn't disrupt a thing, she gave the door a little push.

"Can I help you?"

Crystal jumped straight into the air and turned around so fast she sent the screen door crashing against the old wood siding. A man stood in the shadow of a grove of fruit trees. Her first thought had to do with the self-defense tactics she'd taught that very day. Her second was that the man looked familiar. In fact, he looked like...

"Nathan? Nathan Quinn?"

"Close but no cigar." The man hobbled out of the shadows. "I'm the handsome Quinn, Nathan's brother Marsh." He cast her a smile he'd probably perfected on dozens of unsuspecting females over the years. "You a friend of Nathan's?"

She shook her head. "Not really."

Marsh's grin only grew. "Of course you're not. Who in their right mind would befriend a thick-headed, nearsighted, ornery old bear with a sore paw? You interested in Hester's place?"

As he hobbled closer, she noticed the cast on his leg. "Is Hester here?" she asked.

"She went to the big pink house in the sky three years ago."

Crystal liked this Quinn immediately. "Is it for sale, then?"

"No." He paused, studying her. "But I might be persuaded to rent it if the right person came along. Go on in and take a look."

Crystal didn't need a second invitation. She entered a foyer that contained a steep open stairway and a narrow hallway that led to a small living room and an even smaller kitchen and a dining room that could easily be turned into a place to counsel patients. There was an enchanting half bath tucked beneath the stairs. The only full bathroom was on the second floor, which also contained two bedrooms, one done in red rosebud wallpaper, the other in pink. The third story consisted of a long, narrow room that had a sloped ceiling, some old trunks and windows on either end.

Crystal glanced out one of them and was surprised to see a horse tethered to the back porch, and two men talking down below. Their chins were both set, their shoulders firmly back. There was no mistaking the family resemblance between the two men. Both wore brown cowboy hats. The one not wearing a cast on his leg had to be Nathan Quinn.

Intrigued, she would have liked to study him a little more closely. Instead, she backed away from the window. After counting to twenty, she made a second, more thorough pass through the house. By the time she reached the bottom of the stairs, Marsh and Nathan were nodding their heads and shaking their fists as if in complete agreement over something.

"I could throttle that little brother of ours," Marsh grumbled. "Just once I'd like to know what the hell he's thinking."

Sweeping his hat off his head and raking his fingers through his hair, Nathan said, "Then maybe you'd better go get Holly and let me deal with Zack. Did the doctor say it's okay to drive with that cast?"

"I made the trip from Texas, didn't I?"

Nathan appeared as surprised by Marsh's resentful tone of voice as Crystal was. "Nathan wasn't implying that you weren't capable, Marsh."

Both men turned their heads as she strode onto the porch. "As indicated by his body language, he asked out of concern. He'd lowered his shoulders and leaned toward you in what was probably brotherly concern for your comfort and well-being."

"You got all of that from one line?" Marsh asked.

Before she could reply, Nathan said, "What is she doing here?"

Crystal glanced from one brother to the other. Strolling closer, she reached into her pocket and drew out two business cards. She handed the first to Marsh. "It looks as if you two have issues. If you'd like to resolve them, I can help. I teach communication skills to husbands, wives, families, neighbors and friends. The first visit is free."

She handed the second card to Nathan. The instant her fingers brushed his, he jerked his hand back. The card fluttered to the ground where it settled in the tall weeds with a soft swish. Crystal's gaze settled on Nathan's. For the span of one heartbeat, something powerful passed between their gazes, something that left her warm and made him shift from one foot to the other.

"What is it you said you're doing here?" he asked.

His gaze probed hers. It wasn't often that Crystal couldn't read a man's expression or decipher the underlying meaning in the tone of his voice. "This house is for rent, isn't it?"

"Yes," Marsh said.

"Since when?" Nathan made a conscious effort not to grimace. He knew he'd spoken too loudly, too vehemently. Crystal Galloway had this effect on him. He'd been trying to put her out of his mind all evening. And he didn't want her living in his house. Okay, technically, it was Marsh's house, but it was on Quinn land, a stone's throw from the Quinn homestead.

"Since when is the Mulberry place for rent?" This time his voice was more in control.

"Since about fifteen minutes ago. Do you have a problem with that?"

Nathan glanced from his brown-eyed brother to the green-eyed woman he couldn't seem to get out of his mind. He took his time cramming his hat back on his head. Slowly he began to back up. "I have enough problems, Marsh. If you'll pick up Holly, I'll go see about Zack."

With a nod at Crystal, Nathan mounted his horse.

"Hey, Nathan?" Marsh called.

Nathan finished turning the horse toward home before glancing down at his brother.

"This cast is cumbersome, but I can drive okay. You don't have to worry about Holly."

Watching as the brothers exchanged a nod, Crystal revised her earlier assessment. They communicated just fine, not with words, perhaps, but with nods and gestures and body language.

"Is your brother always like this?" she asked when Nathan was out of hearing range.

"He's been surly all day. I figure it's a good sign."

"A good sign for what?" Crystal asked.

"He got real quiet after Mary died. Their girl, Holly, did, too."

"He's Holly Quinn's father?"

"You know Holly?"

As Nathan and his horse disappeared around a bend, Crystal asked, "Do you ever answer a question?"

"Do you?" Marsh had yet to look at her, his gaze still on the rolling landscape and the land that seemed to stretch for miles. "Three hundred dollars."

"I beg your pardon?" she asked.

"Three hundred dollars. That's what I've decided to charge."

"It goes against my better judgment to ask, but three hundred dollars for what?"

She thought she detected the beginning of a smile at the corners of his mouth. "To rent Hester's old house."

"I thought you said the house was yours."

"On paper it is. Three hundred."

Somewhere a bird started to twitter. A robin, perhaps, or some other warbler. "Three hundred dollars a week?"

"No, a month."

"For the entire house?"

He finally faced her. "You're probably right. Okay, two seventy-five."

She only blinked.

A devilish light entered his eyes. "Two-fifty is about as low as I care to go."

"Two hundred and fifty dollars. Per month. To live in this house."

"Damn." Marsh threw up his hands. "You drive a hard bargain. Fine. Two hundred. That doesn't include utilities."

When she remained silent he said, "What's the matter? Change your mind?"

She studied him in a manner that wasn't considered polite. And then she studied the house. "Are there bats in the belfry, rats in the basement? Is it haunted?"

"It doesn't have a basement or a belfry. And ghosts are afraid of me."

Crystal smiled. "Of course they are. Mind if I ask why you're willing to let it go so cheap?"

"Shoot, doll, I would have let you live here for free just to watch the sparks fly off my brother. Do we have a deal?" He held out his hand.

She glanced in the direction Nathan had gone. "I'm going to have to get back to you, Mr. Quinn."

"Fair enough, but my offer stands. It's yours if you want it."

He'd left his hand where it was, as if daring her to try an experiment. For reasons she chose not to examine too closely, she placed her hand in his. His handshake was warm, his grip strong, his palm slightly rough. Finally she looked up at him. He was watching her, his gaze direct and as steady as his handshake.

"You noticed it, too," he said.

"Noticed what?"

He shrugged and smiled that hundred-watt grin that probably had most women groveling at his feet. "There are no sparks. At least not between you and me. So it isn't the family. It's the man. More specifically, the other man." He winked. "There's no accounting for taste, I suppose, but things sure are getting interesting around here. Now, if you'll excuse me, I have to drive into town to pick up my niece." Without another word, he hobbled toward a rusty pickup truck parked along the side of the road.

Interesting? she wondered, as she made her way through the overgrown yard to her car. Complicated was more like it.

She felt a little surge of excitement mixed with wariness, because once upon a time *complications* might as well have been her middle name.

Chapter Two

Nathan gripped the shifting lever hard. And winced in pain. After downshifting more carefully, he eased up on the gas a little and brought his hand, blood-soaked towel and all, to rest on his thigh. The cut on his hand and this subsequent trip into town were just two more complications on a day that had gone steadily from bad to worse.

He'd turned in late last night and hadn't slept well, only to awaken at six to a shouting match between his two youngest brothers. He knew Ethan meant well, but rubbing Zack's nose in guilt hadn't worked in the past and probably wouldn't in the future. It sure hadn't worked today. They'd put a lid on it when Holly showed up for breakfast. The second she caught the bus for school, Nathan sent them in opposite directions, Ethan to drop off salt licks for the herd and Zack to mend fences on the eastern property line. They'd parted company, sulking, which had been a whole lot easier to deal with than Marsh's annoying I-know-something-you-don't-know grin.

At the last minute Marsh, who was only home temporarily while his broken ankle healed, had decided to ride shotgun with Zack. Which had left Nathan alone when he'd discovered a mare foaling weeks early. Pain-crazed and inexperienced, the first-time mother had been wild, her labor so advanced there hadn't been time to call Luke Carson, the local vet.

Nathan slowed down in front of the J. G. Animal Clinic. If explaining the reason he wanted Luke to stitch up his hand weren't so complicated, Nathan would have paid his old friend a visit and asked him to do the honors. That way he could have put off a face-to-face encounter with Doc Kincaid's receptionist, a complication if there ever was one.

But Nathan drove on and pulled his truck to the curb in front of the doctor's office on Custer Street, set the brake and turned off the engine. A curtain fluttered in the house across the street before he'd taken three steps. It went without saying that news of his mishap would be all over town by lunchtime, just as it went without saying that he simply didn't need any more complications. He had a daughter to raise, a ranch to run, three infuriating brothers to watch out for, the youngest of whom insisted upon getting into trouble, and the second of whom insisted upon flirting with danger down in Texas. Throwing Crystal Galloway into the equation was like climbing the windmill during a thunderstorm. There were some risks a responsible, mature man simply didn't take.

Alone in his bed last night he'd grappled with the memory of how Crystal had felt in his arms. Any man in that situation would have reacted to any woman so close, so soft, so pretty. It was the situation, that was all, one he'd planned to avoid in the future.

Cradling his injured hand in his good one, he went inside. The cowbell over the door, at odds with the classical music playing softly in the background, brought Crystal Galloway into the waiting area.

So much for best-laid plans.

Her eyes widened as she took in the sight of him standing

in the doorway, the towel wrapped around his hand. "Is that blood deceiving, or is it as bad as it looks?" she asked.

"I wouldn't be here if it wasn't."

She continued toward him, burning up a lot of area for someone who moved so sinuously. Nathan was a little sorry he wasn't standing behind her, where he could have gotten the full effect.

He must have been scowling, which she must have assumed was due to the pain, because she asked, "Do you need to sit down?"

"I just need Doc Kincaid to stitch it up for me."

"Come this way."

When he didn't budge, she studied him even more closely. "Are you certain you don't need to sit down?"

His legs *weren't* fully operational, but it had little to do with the cut on his palm or the loss of blood. Crystal was looking up at him with those almond-shaped green eyes, and it was all he could do to keep from slipping right into them.

When he still didn't move, she asked, "Do you have other injuries?"

He shook his head.

"Then what is it?"

What was it? Criminy, it was the softness in her gaze, the sultriness in her voice. It was the orchestra music on the radio. He took a deep breath, inhaling a flowery, exotic scent that made him want to lean a little closer and breathe it in again. It was her scent, and the way it blended with the smell of lilacs in a glass pitcher on a nearby table. It was the season.

"Nathan? Are you going to be ill?"

The shake of his head served a dual purpose, clearing his brain and answering her question at the same time.

"Just don't faint on me, big guy."

He found himself responding to her humor. He didn't

smile, exactly, but he relaxed enough to say, "Don't worry, I've never fainted in my life."

"Let's keep it that way, shall we?" She placed a hand on his forearm. Warmth radiated up his arm, across his shoulder, through his chest. Right then he faced a fact. It wasn't the season or her scent. It wasn't her humor or the tenderness in her eyes or her touch. It wasn't even that she was a woman, and a pretty one at that.

It was *this* particular woman. Aw, hell.

"Look. My hand got caught between a birthing mare and a nail sticking through the wall. I wouldn't have bothered to come in at all, except—"

"A rusty nail?"

His mouth was still open to finish the portion of his statement she'd interrupted. "Just tell Doc Kincaid I'm here."

"He isn't here."

Nathan swiped his hat off his head with his good hand, thinking he knew he should have asked Luke Carson to stitch him up. "Where is he?"

"He's making a house call. Don't worry. I can page him, and if it's necessary, I will. I have nurse's training, so let's have a look, shall we?"

Her no-nonsense attitude had nurse written all over it. She certainly talked like someone in the medical field, with her "let's" this and "we" that. When she led the way down a narrow hallway, he followed her into a small examination room, his gaze trained on the enticing sway of her hips beneath the soft-looking fabric of a long, straight, knit skirt that was probably in style somewhere but not in Jasper Gulch. It wasn't easy to drag his gaze away.

Placing a hand on his shoulder, she gently propelled him into a chair. Her lips were moving. Unfortunately, he couldn't hear over the roaring din in his ears. He was too busy reacting, his mind too busy conjuring up images that turned her bedside manner into a fantasy in the making.

Leaning close, she unwrapped the towel and lifted it

away from the nasty tear across the meatiest part of his palm. "It looks to me as if the rusty nail came out on top."

Nathan's throat constricted.

She scrubbed and dried her hands, slipped on latex gloves and reached for a jar of brownish-red antiseptic. "We'll just get this wound cleaned up a little before Dr. Kincaid returns. It's a nasty tear. You're right about it needing stitches."

He must have mumbled something agreeable, because she continued talking. And talking. Since it was a lot safer than doing what he was thinking about doing, he listened.

Growing up in a family of men, he'd never quite mastered the fine art of small talk. He was pretty sure women were born with that particular skill. "Burke Kincaid says you're a godsend," he said, trying to keep up his end.

She smiled. "That's because I'm the only person this side of the Rocky Mountains that can read his handwriting."

While she continued to work on his hand, Nathan studied the sweep of her lashes, the exotic tilt of her eyes, the narrow nose and full lips. She'd fastened her long, wavy hair behind her head in some sort of a twisted braid that looked complicated and pretty at the same time. He wondered how difficult it would be to unfasten. "You said you have medical training?" he asked to take his mind off his wayward thoughts.

"Nursing was one of several courses of study I began but didn't quite finish." She pulled a face. "Until two years ago, that is, when I went back and took the exam and passed the state test. I had a little trouble deciding what to be when I grew up. Would you mind keeping that tidbit of information to yourself?"

If she wanted to keep her personal matters private, so be it. "I quit college after only one year, so don't worry, my lips are sealed."

But hers weren't. They were parted slightly, the bottom fuller than the top.

"You didn't like school?" she asked.

He answered by rote. "Let's just say it wasn't for me."

"No regrets?" she asked.

He shifted uncomfortably in his chair. "A few. I didn't come right home after college. Mary and I moved to Aberdeen, where I worked in the mining industry for almost three years. But there was only one thing I ever wanted to be. So Mary and Holly and I came home."

She stopped swabbing his hand with the cold antiseptic and reached for a jar containing large gauze pads. "That's one of the things I envy about the people here. For all their complaining about taxes and floods or droughts and the shortage of women, they're relatively content. They know where they want to be, what they want to do, how they want to live."

"You don't?"

She shrugged offhandedly. "I'm figuring it out as I go."

"Where are you from?"

"I was born in Philadelphia. My parents shipped me off to boarding school as soon as they could. I rebelled. Consequently I was expelled from one school after another, in one state after another. Guess you could say I was an enigma, a classic underachiever with brains I chose not to use. I used to envy people with normal IQs, people who are comfortable in the world and their place in it. People who don't view the world from the outside looking in."

"No brothers, sisters, husbands, kids?"

Something flickered far back in her eyes. She looked away before Nathan could put a label on the emotion.

"I thought I found love once or twice, but ultimately it fizzled."

Crystal glanced down at Nathan, a serious mistake, because she couldn't look away. His gaze was trained on her mouth, which was where a delicious heat started, but not where it ended. It left her feeling charmed and wanted. It was a feeling she'd craved when she was younger, a long time ago.

"Then you came in answer to the ad the local boys placed in the papers a few years back?" he asked.

The warmth inside her radiated outward even as she said, "I saw a follow-up article in a magazine a year later." She paused for a moment, being careful with the wording of the remainder of her explanation. "The timing was right, so I left Albuquerque and moved back to South Dakota. I believe I can do good here, but I didn't move here to find a man, if that's what you're asking." She didn't admit the other reason she'd moved here, not even to herself, until after the decision had been made.

Under normal circumstances Nathan would have been thinking clearly enough to be able to separate that information into categories. But he wasn't thinking clearly. He wasn't thinking, period. He was reacting, perhaps even fantasizing a little....

"Nathan?"

His eyes focused on hers.

"The pain in your hand. Is it okay?"

He heard the question and yet all he could think was, what pain? Hell, what hand? He must have nodded, because she placed his hand over the sterile gauze, showing him how much pressure to apply to the wound.

"I've thought about what you said when you discovered that I was interested in renting that house from your brother, and I'm sorry if I upset you."

Nathan felt his eyes narrowing. Her gaze was downturned, so she failed to notice the change that came over him.

"I didn't know you were Holly Quinn's father. You've been through enough without me adding—"

"Insult to injury?" He jerked his hand out of her grasp and swore at the pain the movement inflicted. Crystal's eyebrows rose fractionally, her gaze sweeping over him. As far as he was concerned, it was a little late to be reading his body language.

"I didn't mean it like that."

Oh, yes, she did. Nathan was ticked. With good reason. He'd been sitting here, responding to her on the most fundamental level, fantasizing about how it would feel to kiss her, and touch her, and be touched by her. And she'd been feeling sorry for him.

He rose slowly to his feet. "I need your pity like I need another gash in my hand. Caring for my wife the two years she was ill doesn't make me a charity case or a saint. You want to do some good, fine. Find someone else to pity."

A knock sounded on the door while Crystal's mouth was still gaping. She opened it, the door, that is, and closed her mouth.

Dr. Kincaid entered the small examination room, only to stare from Crystal to Nathan and back again. Recovering first, Crystal gestured to Nathan's hand. "Mr. Quinn had a little scuffle with a rusty nail."

In his late thirties, Burke Kincaid was dark, like Nathan. But Burke was a city man, born and bred, and Nathan was a rancher from the dent in his cowboy hat to the pointed toes of his boots. Donning a lab coat, Burke walked to the sink where he began scrubbing his hands. The cowbell jangled out in the waiting room. An instant later a child's wails rent the air.

Crystal peeled off her latex gloves and dropped them into a wastebasket, which she opened by pressing a lever with the toe of one shoe. "I'll check on them and be right back, Doctor."

"Go ahead and get the next patient settled. You've gotten everything ready here. I can take care of this cut."

At the door Crystal said, "Do you want to give Mr. Quinn a tetanus shot?"

"Have you had one in the past ten years?" Burke asked Nathan.

Nathan shook his head, shrugged. The good doctor was still scrubbing his hands, so he didn't hear Crystal suggest which size needle to use and where Doc might administer the shot, but Nathan sure heard it.

He also heard the door close just short of a slam.

What an ornery, contrary man!

Crystal stacked the toys in the corner and straightened the magazines in the reception area. She'd gotten Lisa and little Rose McCully settled in the other examining room, then spent the last ten minutes taking phone calls, scheduling appointments, and deciphering Burke's handwriting. And thinking. Lord, yes, she couldn't seem to stop doing that.

She'd become a counselor because she'd wanted to help people deal with their pasts, their grief, perhaps, their sadness, rejections, depressions, issues and failures, not insult them. Oh, but Nathan brought out her temper and raised her hackles. Still, her behavior had been unprofessional. Worse, she'd been nasty, and that was simply uncalled for.

She was trying to decide how to smooth things over when the quiet thud of footsteps drew her gaze. Nathan stood in the doorway, looking at her. He was ruggedly built, his shoulders broad, his shirt and jeans faded, his boots dusty. With his cowboy hat held loosely in his bandaged right hand, he strode directly to the counter where she sat. "They say it's easier to ask for forgiveness than for permission, but I don't think so."

"I was just thinking the same thing."

"You were?" He looked genuinely relieved, but only for a moment. "Look," he said. "My outburst was...shoot, I was out of line. No matter what else Marsh and I disagree about, we both believe a man is only as good as his word.

Since he gave you his word, it's only fair that you rent the Mulberry place if you want to.''

She tilted her head slightly. ''I signed the lease two hours ago, Nathan.''

Only his eyes showed his surprise. ''Then what was the purpose behind that pity party in the examining room?''

''You're the one who mentioned pity.''

He shook his head as if he knew full well he'd over-reacted. ''You're probably thinking I could use my head examined.''

''I could recommend a counselor if you'd like.''

His dark eyebrows drew together, forming a straight line. ''I thought you said you were a counselor.''

''I am, but I'm afraid it would be unethical for me to counsel you, after all.''

''Unethical?'' Nathan didn't know why he'd asked. He didn't even want a counselor, dammit.

''The counselor-patient relationship wouldn't work between us.''

He was becoming accustomed to the intelligence in Crystal's eyes. She said a lot in only a few words. It kept him on his toes. ''I suppose you have a reason.''

She glanced around as if to make sure the coast was clear, then rose to her feet. Holding his gaze, she said, ''I'm afraid my attraction to you would get in the way of my ability to remain focused and think clearly.''

Nathan had to clench his teeth to keep his mouth from falling open. There wasn't anything he could do about the heat pooling low in his body. A beautiful woman had just admitted that she was attracted to him. Criminy and Holy Moses.

''I'm sorry, Nathan.''

Just then the cowbell jangled again, signaling another patient's arrival. Taking advantage of the distraction, he dropped some cash on the counter and left.

* * *

All three of his brothers were in the barn when Nathan pulled the Jeep inside and got out. Marsh and Ethan seemed to be in good spirits. Zack was sulking, sitting in the hayloft, his feet dangling over the edge.

"Where's Holly?" Ethan asked.

"She's spending the night at Jenna's."

"Oh, man," Ethan complained. "That means one of us has to cook. I sure wish I had a woman to do that."

A horse neighed on the other side of the barn. Marsh snorted. "If that's the only use you can think of for a woman, it's no wonder you're still as pure as the driven snow."

"Who says I'm pure?"

Nathan lifted a saddle from the rack and heaved it onto Montego's broad back.

"You saying you're not?" Marsh asked, climbing carefully off the gate he'd been sharing with Ethan.

"I don't kiss and tell," Ethan declared.

Marsh made a clucking noise. Nathan noticed that Zack almost grinned. He hoped it was a good sign.

"What are you doing?" Marsh asked, when it was obvious that Nathan was saddling up his favorite horse.

"I'm taking Montego out and letting him run off some steam."

Hopping off the gate in one smooth jump, Ethan started toward him. "Who's going to cook supper?"

Nathan held up his bandaged right hand. "I have doctor's orders to keep this dry."

"I guess we vote," Marsh said. "I say Zack can cook supper."

"Kiss my—"

Nathan glanced at Marsh, half expecting his younger brother to tell Zack what he could do with his attitude. Instead, Marsh turned to Ethan. "Looks like you're cooking."

"What?" Ethan sputtered.

"Are you deaf or dumb?" Marsh said in that infuriating voice he had.

The two younger Quinns shared a look. As if by unspoken agreement, Ethan faced Marsh, and Zack made his way toward the ladder.

"You know," Ethan said, "I've never liked his condescending attitude."

Nathan finished tightening the cinch. When Marsh took a backward step, Nathan smiled to himself.

"Me, neither," Zack said, blithely climbing out of the hayloft.

"Think we ought to teach him a lesson?" Ethan asked Zack.

Even though Marsh said, "It wouldn't be a fair fight," he took another backward step.

"Every man for himself," Ethan declared.

"Loser cooks dinner," Zack said as he lunged for his second oldest brother, his hat flying off his head, his shaggy hair falling into his face.

"Watch the cast!" Marsh said moments before he hit the ground.

They rolled through the open door and landed on the grass in a heap. Shaking his head at the sight of his brothers wrestling the way they had years ago, Nathan had half a mind to join them. A good hard roll on the ground would go a long way in relieving the tension that had been coiled tight in his gut for the past two days. A good hard roll in the hay with a certain blonde would be a helluva lot more fun.

He hooked a foot in the stirrup and swung onto Montego's back. A good hard run on his favorite horse was going to have to suffice. "Try not to hurt each other," he called.

"Getting hurt got you out of cooking!" Ethan called a moment before Zack wiggled out from the bottom of the heap and pinned Ethan.

Of course, it was only a matter of seconds before Marsh pried him off and the fight continued. Nathan pointed Montego toward the lane. Behind him oomphs and ughs were exchanged along with an occasional ear-singeing cuss word. Chances were slim that any of them would be preparing supper anytime soon.

Man and horse crossed Sugar Creek at the shallowest point. After scaling the other bank, they broke into a run. From there it was only a matter of a hundred yards before they came to the vine-covered stone fence Nathan's great-grandfather had built with his own two hands sixty years ago. There was no sense pretending he hadn't known he would end up here.

Easing the horse to a slower pace, Nathan eyed the pink house and overgrown yard. Pale-pink blush, his great-aunt Hester had called it. He saw the car right away. It took him a few seconds to find the woman amidst the boxes stacked on the porch.

She strode to the railing, shading her eyes with one hand.

The knot inside him coiled tighter. For lack of a better plan, he dismounted. "Ethan said you were moving in," he called.

"How many more brothers do you have?"

"Just one you haven't met. Zack."

"Ah, yes, the one Marsh wanted to throttle the other night."

"That's some memory you have." He led Montego through an area in the fence where the rocks had crumbled, then tethered him to a low mulberry branch.

"That's some horse you have," she said.

Montego whinnied. Nathan said, "He likes you, too."

"How can you tell?"

"Trust me, I know." Leaving the horse to graze, Nathan strode closer.

"Is he the father of that baby horse you helped deliver yesterday?"

"Montego's a gelding. But don't tell him."

"You don't think he knows?"

He paused at the edge of the porch, one foot on the lowest step. He was close enough to see her smile. Close enough to see the bright red toenail polish peeking between the straps of her sandals. And everything in between. Her shorts were light-blue, not baggy, not tight. She leaned down, sinuous and graceful, the action drawing his gaze to a pair of long, slim legs. Hoisting a cardboard box into her hands, she stood up.

"Might as well make yourself useful," she said about a second before she hefted the carton into his good hand, leaving him little choice but to take it. While he ascended the steps, she reached for a second, smaller box, which she carried inside.

He put the box next to hers on the old kitchen counter. Opening the lid of the larger of the two, she began to remove a cappuccino machine, a coffee grinder, a pepper grinder, assorted can openers, both hand-held and electric, several nutcrackers, a melon baller and a few utensils he'd never seen before.

Lifting an unusual-looking item from the second box, he said, "An electric card shuffler?"

She shrugged. "I like gadgets."

He couldn't tell if she was serious.

"I'm nothing if not honest, Nathan."

Her uncanny ability to read him was unsettling. "Then you meant what you said earlier."

She opened the lid on another box and moved stuff around inside. "I always mean what I say."

"In that case, would you mind telling me what you meant when you said you're sorry?"

"I beg your pardon?"

Her hands full of baking utensils, she leaned down and

dumped the paraphernalia into a low drawer. Her shirt was long-sleeved, not overtly sexy or revealing, the neckline just low enough to give him a momentary glimpse of the upper swell of one pale, full breast.

Nathan cleared his throat and looked elsewhere. "When you apologized in the doctor's office today. Did you mean you're sorry you can't counsel me? Or are you sorry you're attracted to me."

She closed the drawer, waiting to answer until after she'd straightened. "Would you be offended if I said both?"

"Hell, lady, I'd be relieved."

Their gazes met, held. The smile they shared was slow in coming, wide-spreading, far-reaching.

Just then, a loud whoop carried on the still evening air. "What was that?" She peered out the open kitchen window. "A bird?"

"Not a bird."

She meandered out to the porch, where she said, "Some animal, then?"

"In a sense, I suppose. My brothers are on the warpath."

Her quizzical expression brought on another smile. Talking to her wasn't easy. Staying ahead of her required skill. It felt good to be the one on the understanding end of the conversation. "Marsh, Ethan and Zack are wrestling to see who cooks supper."

"Wrestling?"

He shrugged. "You know, roughhousing."

"Aren't they a little old to be doing that?"

"Marsh is thirty-six. Ethan's thirty, and Zack's twenty-eight. Age isn't a factor. Didn't your father ever horse around?"

"My father didn't play. He read."

"What about your mother?"

She fiddled with the lid on another box, but instead of carrying it inside, she strode to the far end of the porch and studied the horizon. "My father was fifty-seven when I was born. My mother was twelve years younger. I know people who are those ages and who are extremely young, but I don't think my parents ever were. They always seemed ancient to me.''

"Are they both gone now?''

"My father is. My mother lives in Phoenix. We're not close.''

"It's too bad you didn't have brothers or sisters.''

"I once made the mistake of asking my mother for a baby sister. The poor woman nearly had an embolism. I think she was horrified enough because she had to deal with evidence that she and my father had shared a bed at least once.''

She pulled a face, and Nathan nodded in understanding. "It's never easy to imagine our parents, well, you know what I mean.''

He'd been imagining himself in some pretty stimulating fantasies, though. Getting back on track, he said, "They didn't have a loving relationship?''

She strolled to the steps, then lowered to the top one. Nathan did the same.

"Let's see. How did my mother put it? They were fond of each other.''

Nathan uttered an unbecoming word. "I'm fond of my horse.''

Crystal glanced at the big, powerful animal, which happened to be grazing on the flat of petunias she'd purchased but hadn't planted yet. "I'm fond of my living room sofa.''

"Birdsong in early morning.''

"The way the sunlight streams through the windows in this house.''

He stretched his legs out on the grass below. "Winning an argument with Marsh.''

"Winning an argument with anyone.''

They turned their heads in the same instant. And broke out laughing. His gaze strayed to her mouth, and their laughter trailed away. He shifted on the step. She crossed her arms. Neither action seemed to do much to dispel the attraction that had a way of coming out of nowhere between them.

He was the first to look away. Staring out at the over-grown yard, and beyond where whoops and hollers no longer carried on the breeze, she said, "Who do you think won?"

"Probably Marsh. He cheats."

"That charming man cheats?"

"You think Marsh is charming?"

With a wide sweep of both hands she gestured to the house and tiny yard. "He rented this place to me, didn't he?"

Nathan nodded. "Somehow we've gotten off on the wrong foot."

Crystal sensed another apology was forthcoming. Holding up one hand, she said, "It was no more your fault than mine, Nathan." Her gaze fell to the worn wedding band on his left hand. "You have your reasons. To tell you the truth, I've been burned and am not looking to repeat the process, either."

"I'm trying to decide where that leaves us."

She assumed a pondering position, one arm folded at her waist, the other cupping her chin as if lost in thought. "It doesn't look as if we're going to be lovers." He moved so suddenly his leather boots creaked in protest. Crystal hid a smile. The poor man wasn't accustomed to her little tendency to say what she was thinking at the exact moment she was thinking it. "And we won't be therapist and patient," she said. "I guess we'll have to settle for being neighbors."

She looked up at him, but his expression was impossible to read beneath the shadow of his brown Stetson. Neighbors, she added to herself, who just happened to have an unholy attraction to each other.

She noticed the bandage on his hand. Curious, she asked, "How many stitches did you end up with?"

"Seven."

"Seven's lucky. What did the mare have?"

He gave her one of those questioning looks people gave her a lot. "What mare?"

"The one who was pain crazed and whose labor was too advanced to give you time to call the vet. Did she have a boy or a girl?"

"She had a filly." A long stretch of silence followed. Finally he said, "You're welcome to stop over and see her sometime."

She almost told him that his excitement underwhelmed her, but decided to let it go.

"I should be getting back."

"And I should be getting back to my unpacking."

He found his feet, ambling away with a walk that simply had to be legendary. After swinging a foot over his horse's broad back, he adjusted the reins and rode away.

Suddenly Crystal felt very alone.

She told herself it was just because she was trying to get settled into a new house. Change was always difficult.

Returning to the stack of boxes, she reminded herself that she had a full life, friends, reasons to get up every morning and go to bed every night. She carted a box labeled Bedroom upstairs to the red rosebud room. She'd moved several times over the years. Much of her belongings were in storage, therefore there hadn't been a lot to move from the old-fashioned boarding house where she'd been living since coming to Jasper Gulch. There were a few personal items she'd kept with her wherever she went.

She opened the box containing the most cherished of them and automatically reached for a square object wrapped in tissue paper. Carefully she unfolded the layers of paper and lifted a photograph in a pewter frame. She sat on the edge of the bed, staring at the picture of the most beautiful baby she'd ever seen. The child, a girl with round cheeks, little wisps of fine, blond hair, a button nose and a contagious grin that lit up her entire face, held a pickle in one hand. A fistful of birthday cake was squashed in her other hand. She was wearing a ruffled, powder-blue dress and was sitting in a highchair, grinning for the camera.

Other than the picture Crystal carried in her memory and in her heart, this was the only photograph she had. She hadn't actually seen her or held her or rocked her or kissed her since she'd walked out of the hospital alone, tears coursing down her face fifteen years ago, a year before this photo had arrived in the mail via the attorney's office.

It could have been taken in any diner in any small town anywhere. There were faded red gingham curtains at the window, a snow-covered old lamppost out front, a saloon across the street, part of a sign, the letters *C-r-a-z-y H* visible over the door.

Not a day had gone by that Crystal hadn't thought about that child. But she hadn't given that diner or the view outside its window much thought. Until she saw it in a magazine article a year and a half ago.

On the front page of the article was a photo of three smiling, newly married couples sitting around a table in a local diner. Beneath the picture was the caption The Brides and Grooms of Bachelor Gulch. Heart racing, Crystal had stared at the photograph, then carried it to her nightstand to compare it to the photo of the baby. The same red-checked curtains hung at the same window. It was the same lamppost, the same saloon across the street.

She hadn't been able to stop thinking about that article, that town, those people. She'd arrived in Jasper Gulch without a clear-cut plan. She'd been accused of being impulsive. God knows it had gotten her into trouble when she was young. But the impulse to come here was different. She'd walked the quaint streets, met the shy but willing Jasper Gents, lunched in that diner. And she'd stayed. She hadn't

come here to find a husband. Above all else, she hadn't
moved here to go back on her word or break her promise.

Shortly after she'd settled in, she'd overheard two members of the Ladies Aid Society, which, as far as Crystal was
concerned was just a glorified name for gossips, talking
about a couple and their adopted daughter who'd lived in
Jasper Gulch for a few years but now lived in Murdo, a
small town twenty-five miles away. It might have been the
same child. What were the chances that two families in a
town this small had adopted baby girls?

Crystal had decided that maybe it was better this way.
Twenty-five miles wasn't that far for a grown girl to go if
she ever decided to search for her birth mother. And if she
didn't, twenty-five miles might as well be twenty-five thousand.

At least this way Crystal didn't scan every face she met
for similarities and traits she might recognize. That didn't
mean she didn't harbor a secret hope, a quiet yearning....

Sighing, she placed the frame on the table next to the
bed, only to stride to the window, lost in thought. The sun
was setting, the last rays of light casting a golden glow on
the large house in the distance where Nathan Quinn lived
with his brothers and daughter. The mulberry bushes obstructed the view from downstairs, but up here she could
see for miles. The house was only a quarter of a mile away,
not far at all by country standards. Knowing they were
there, a stone's throw away, made her feel less lonely,
somehow. Maybe she would walk over tomorrow to see
that filly he'd mentioned. She thought about the wedding
band Nathan still wore and the attraction he was fighting.

She looked out the window at the Quinn homestead
again. Returning to the boxes, she got to work.

Chapter Three

A wrapper swirled on a miniwhirlwind as Crystal rounded the corner at Maple Street and ducked into the alley behind her friend's antiques and fine furnishings store. That same spring breeze tugged at her clothes and tore at the hair secured in a loose knot at her nape. A sudden gust slipped through the back door right along with her, sending nearly a dozen wind chimes purling high in the rafters.

"Close the door, quick!" Holly Quinn whispered, peeking out of the back room. "Those chimes will wake the baby."

Crystal closed the door as quietly as possible before tiptoeing to the doorway of the room Sky and Meredith Buchanan had converted into a nursery shortly after their baby had been born in January. Holly was peering over a portable crib. Holding her breath, Crystal waited for the verdict, which came in the form of a thumbs-up sign and a big smile. Four-and-a-half-month-old Storm Buchanan was still sound asleep.

"Where's Meredith?" Crystal mouthed.

Holly waited to answer until she and Crystal were out in

the main portion of the store where the antique sofas, chests and lamps were arranged. "She left me in charge while she ran across the street to the grocery store to pick up some teething gel for Stormy."

Crystal automatically glanced over her shoulder at the corner of the crib that was visible through the doorway. "Do babies teethe so young?"

"Must be."

An eleventh grader, Holly was nearly the same height as Crystal, which was taller than most of the girls here. Her hair was an unusual color, too, like wheat fields in August. Crystal had been pudgy throughout her teens. Holly complained that she was too thin. Girls, Crystal thought. She had a soft spot for them, no doubt about it.

Holly strolled around the room, running her hand across the ornate trim on a beautiful old armoire. More often than not these days, Holly's lips wore a smile, which was a far cry from the way she'd been when Crystal first met her six months ago, only eight months after the death of the girl's beloved mother. Until recently, Crystal hadn't known any of the other Quinns. Now, it seemed they were coming out of the woodwork, strolling over or popping in on her when she least expected. All except Nathan, that is. She hadn't seen him since he'd ridden away four nights ago. But she'd heard about him from each of his brothers. They all respected him and were secretly worried about him. She'd picked up bits and pieces about Mary, too.

"Oh, that woman could cook," Ethan had exclaimed. "Man, I miss that." It was easy to read between those lines. Ethan Quinn missed a lot more than his sister-in-law's cooking.

"I think Nathan would marry again if he could find a woman like Mary." That had come from Zack, the youngest and most disreputable looking, with his shaggy hair and rare grins.

Sweet Mary, Marsh had called her.

Sweet was one word no one had ever used to describe Crystal.

She hadn't seen or heard from Nathan himself. Which, as far as she was concerned, was extremely telling. She hadn't seen much of Holly, either.

"Holly, is something wrong?"

The girl answered without turning around. "I've been invited to be a guest, along with several other young musicians from across the country, of the Boston Symphony Orchestra. And I've been trying to talk to my dad about it for days."

"What are you waiting for?"

"The right time, I guess, but time's running out. I don't want to upset him, and I know he hates it when I talk about leaving Jasper Gulch, but it's only for a week, and it's an experience of a lifetime, something I would never forget."

Crystal had a sudden memory of bright lights that shone on musicians all dressed in black, and her, all dressed in pink, sitting between her mother and father in the audience. She'd been nine years old, and so excited to be allowed to spend an evening with her parents. She sat up, straight and still, not moving a muscle even though her feet didn't touch the floor. It hadn't been easy to keep from fidgeting and squirming, but she'd tried her hardest to be a good, obedient little girl. She'd done well, too. Right up until intermission when she'd tripped over her own sleeping foot and fallen flat on her face. She'd bloodied her nose and stained her pretty pink dress. Worse, she'd made a spectacle of herself. Those had been her mother's exact words. As usual, her father hadn't uttered a sound.

"Uncle Zack says you give great advice." Holly's voice brought Crystal back to the present. "And I was sort of hoping you might have a few pointers for me."

Crystal spoke softly. "I don't have magic up my sleeve, Holly. Your dad strikes me as an honorable man. I suggest you talk to him. Be honest and open."

Holly pulled a face. "That's it? I'm doomed."

Out of the blue, a thought occurred to Crystal. She couldn't help smiling as she passed it on. "You could try feeding him first."

Holly's blue eyes crinkled at the corners, the freckles on her nose making her look happy, suddenly, and just a little conniving. Just then the bell over the front door jangled, announcing the arrival of a customer. "I'd better see who that is."

Crystal glanced at her watch, gauging how much time she had before Pamela Sue and Grover Andrews were due to arrive at her house for their counseling session. She was organizing her notes when the baby let out his first squawk.

Crystal held perfectly still.

She'd been Meredith's labor coach last winter and had been present when the baby made his debut. Witnessing the miracle of Storm Buchanan's birth had nearly turned Crystal inside out. Afterward, she'd taken a close look at her life and at what she was doing with it. It was then that she'd decided to open her counseling practice in Jones County. She'd also organized a youth group and started a communications workshop for people of all ages. Life was short, and she'd decided it was time to stop wasting a minute of it.

The baby was crying with gusto now. Meredith craned her neck to see to the front of the store. Holly had turned a paint-mixing machine on, and appeared to be busy talking to Forest Wilkie.

Oh, dear.

Storm's face was red, his arms flailing, his chubby fingers curled into fists. Crystal understood the splitting of atoms and the policies of several dozen foreign countries. But she knew nothing about babies.

Oh, dear, oh, dear, oh, dear.

She'd been touched and honored when Meredith and Sky had asked her to be Storm's godmother. She'd held him a few times while he'd been sleeping. Awake, he scared her. Crying, he terrified her.

She slunk a little closer, easing a hand over the edge of the crib. "There, there," she murmured. "Don't cry."

He turned his head toward her voice, his tears her undoing. Heart racing, she slipped the strap of her purse over her shoulder and slid her hands around the baby. He felt so warm. So small. So fragile. Shaking slightly, she picked him up as if he were made of glass.

His cries lessened in intensity, stilling completely once he was in an upright position. It was as if he didn't know that she had no idea what she was doing. Or he didn't care.

"You got what you wanted, didn't you?" she whispered around the lump in her throat, her lips close to his delicate little ear.

Just in case he started to cry again, she strolled to the front of the store so she would be closer to Holly, an experienced baby-sitter. Storm was quiet as she said hello to Forest. So far so good. She meandered around the area where the new furniture was arranged, steering clear of anything she might trip over. And then she did something she tried not to do. She breathed in the scent of baby powder and innocence, of a little shirt washed in special soap, and sweetness beyond description. It transported her back in time, making her ache in a place beneath her heart, a place she'd never been able to name.

The bell jangled again. In one corner of her mind, she was aware that Meredith had returned. She heard her friend exchange small talk with Forest, but she didn't turn around until a third voice, this one a deep, masculine baritone, joined the conversation.

It was uncanny the way her gaze seemed to meet Nathan's so unerringly from so many feet away.

"Hello, Crystal."

It was unnerving how a simple hello could make her feel weak in the knees.

"I hardly believe it," Meredith said, hurrying toward her. "You're holding Storm!"

Suddenly Crystal remembered that she was inept. She stiffened up, which startled the baby, who started to cry all over again. "You can see how much he likes it," she said, handing the squalling infant into his mother's waiting arms.

Meredith kissed her son's little cheek. "It isn't you. He's been fretful all day. I think he's trying to cut a tooth."

Jiggling the baby, Meredith struck up a conversation with Forest. Crystal had forgotten he was even there. It was strange, because she was aware of Nathan's slightest move. Just being in the same room with him sent anticipation and a heady sense of urgency racing through her.

Holly grabbed her backpack and waved goodbye to Meredith. Mouthing the words "wish me luck" she practically glided out the door her father was holding.

Crystal felt a click in her mind. It lasted no longer than the flash of a camera, and made her feel as if she'd glimpsed something familiar. Nathan glanced at her, and Crystal swallowed, realizing that what was familiar was the connection arcing from his gaze to hers. It was a connection he fought. Was it because he wasn't ready? Or was it because she was nothing like his late wife?

She didn't like feeling inept. She liked feeling vulnerable even less. She turned away from the window before she did something impulsive and brash, like winking, or batting her eyelashes, something kind, sweet Mary probably wouldn't have done in a million years. Something else clicked in her brain, and all the years she'd spent trying to be what someone else wanted her to be came crashing around her, stopping her in her tracks.

She was who she was. Either a person liked her for it or didn't.

She swung around and hurried through the door. "Nathan?" Maybe her behavior was brash. Maybe she was being impulsive. At least she was being true to herself.

Nathan closed the door for Holly, automatically rounding the front of the truck. Crystal was moseying closer, the breeze toying with the hem of her skirt, a smile toying with her mouth.

He'd seen the light in her windows at night, her car in the driveway at lunchtime, but he hadn't seen her up close in days. She'd ignored the invitation to visit the ranch and see the new filly. Which was fine with him. It wasn't as if he'd asked her for a date. Hell, he was so out of practice, he wasn't even sure how men went about asking women out for dates anymore.

"I suppose I could have called you about this later," she said.

Huh. Marsh claimed women did the asking half the time these days. Nathan liked the sound of this.

"Since you're here," she continued, "I thought I'd talk to you about this now."

He liked it a lot. "What's on your mind, Crystal?"

She looked at him a little strangely for a moment, as if she didn't understand why he suddenly sounded so lofty. She glanced to the right of his shoulder, smiled, probably at Holly, then looked at him again. "I just wanted you to know that I'd be more than happy to give Holly a ride home on the days her work schedule at the store coincides with mine."

Just like that the breeze died away, taking Nathan's loftiness with it. "You want to give Holly a ride home?"

"It's no trouble. When I'm going that way, anyway, I might as well be neighborly."

How the hell could he argue with that logic? How the hell could he refuse? Why would he want to refuse?

"Sure. Okay. That's right nice of you." He clamped his lips together and gritted his teeth.

She waved at Holly, looked slightly askance at him, then returned to the store. If he'd been paying attention, he would have noticed her secret, knowing, infuriating little smile. But Nathan was too busy trying to remember what decade anybody had last said, "That's right nice of you," to notice anything except his own dark mood.

Nathan stood at the top of the porch steps, ankles crossed, one shoulder leaning on a post. It had gotten dark a while ago; he'd lost track of time, but if he breathed deeply enough, he could still smell the chicken and dumplings Holly had prepared for supper.

He'd reconciled himself to the fact that he'd made a fool of himself with Crystal today. But he couldn't seem to get the image of her holding that baby out of his mind. Until this afternoon he'd seen her as a goddess, an enchantress, a fantasy in the making. Today she'd looked so soft, so enraptured, so sad.

He'd never come across a woman he understood less and who drew him more. Not that he was about to admit that out loud. He'd be darned if he would join the ranks of everyone else around here who dropped Crystal's name into every conversation.

It was Crystal this and Crystal that.

Did he know that Crystal played the oboe? Nathan wasn't positive what an oboe sounded like. It was another woodwind instrument, wasn't it?

She'd introduced Ethan to cappuccino when everybody knew cowboys drank plain coffee, strong and black. She ground her own pepper. She'd signed Marsh's cast in flowing, loopy handwriting that reminded Nathan of her every time he saw it. She'd played cards with Zack, who insisted he'd never seen anybody who could shuffle a deck of cards the way she could. She'd taught him a thing or two. As far as Nathan was concerned, if Zack paid more attention to ranching and less to poker, he wouldn't be in the mess he was in, and he wouldn't have an appointment with a judge in Murdo tomorrow. In all fairness, Zack's drunk-and-disorderly charge had nothing to do with Crystal. She was just being friendly.

To him she was neighborly.

Nathan felt like chewing glass.

"Hey, Daddy."

He looked over his shoulder as Holly joined him on the porch. "Hi, shortcake."

"You thinking about Mom?"

Nathan shrugged noncommittally, feeling guilty suddenly, because the woman he'd been thinking about hadn't been Mary.

"That was some supper you fixed us."

"I thought Uncle Marsh was going to eat until he exploded." She giggled, and Nathan was reminded of earlier years when she'd giggled a lot.

She sat down on the porch swing, folding one leg underneath her, looping her arms around the other. When she'd been little, she'd reminded him of a fawn, all wobbly legs and round eyes. She was five-seven now. Much to her annoyance and disappointment, she hadn't filled out the way she wanted. She was still all legs and eyes, his little girl.

Warmth started in his chest as he joined her on the swing. Spending time with his little girl was exactly what he needed tonight. He set the swing in motion, and she started to talk. Ethan called it prattle. Nathan had forgotten how much he'd missed it. She told him how she'd prepared supper, what seasonings she'd used, what she was studying in chemistry class. She was getting straight As, except for a bothersome A- in calculus, which as far as Nathan was concerned wasn't even math. "I'm proud of you, honey. You always do your best."

The swing swayed to and fro. "I try really hard."

"Yes, you do."

"You and Mom always encouraged me to get extra help if it means I can do better."

He nodded, feeling the slightest bit drowsy. A hard day's work followed by a good meal, a warm spring night, the gentle sway of a porch swing, his daughter's easy chatter. Any minute now his chin was going to tip forward, coming to rest on his chest. If he wasn't careful, he would be snoring softly soon.

"Hear that?" Holly asked. "Crystal's playing her flute."

"Hmmm." He'd noticed an occasional twitter of musical notes on the evening breeze.

"Crystal plays the piano, too, and the oboe, and the harp."

Somewhere in Nathan's mind, a thought swirled. Crystal this and Crystal that.

"I've never heard anyone play like her," Holly said. "Well, at least not anybody I actually know. She took lessons for fifteen years, studying under teachers she called maestros. Do you think I'll ever be that good?"

"There aren't too many maestros around here, but if you keep working at it, I don't see any reason—"

"Not here, maybe, but in Boston, there sure are."

"I suppose so." His eyes drifted closed.

"And it would be a shame to pass up any opportunity to improve, wouldn't it, Daddy?"

Nathan sat up a little straighter. "I guess."

"That's exactly what I told Mrs. Carson you would say. You would never want me to pass up an opportunity of a lifetime. And that's what sitting in on a dress rehearsal of the Boston Symphony Orchestra would be."

"The Boston Symphony Orchestra?"

"Uh-huh."

"In Boston?" All at once, he was wide awake.

Before he knew how it happened, she'd kissed him on the cheek and told him she knew he would understand, and she was just sure that once he'd thought about it, he would agree that the invitation she'd received to go to Boston was indeed the opportunity of a lifetime.

"Of course, I don't expect an answer right away. You'll want to think about it. You're the best, Daddy."

She batted those golden eyelashes of hers and looked at him with those big, blue, round eyes, then hurried inside on those fawn legs. It was then that Nathan faced the fact that she was no longer a fawn, but a doe. She'd fed him and used her feminine wiles to lure him into a false sense of security, then *bam!*

His little girl was growing up.

The sweet, clear, fine-toned notes of another instrument carried on the still evening air. Nathan leaned toward it the way the children had in the old fable "The Pied Piper." He was becoming accustomed to the heaviness that had a way of settling to the very center of him when he least expected, but feeling like a bandy-legged tenderfoot again was going to take a little getting used to.

He had the good sense to admit that it had to do with his new neighbor. He scowled. His new neighbor, who was warm and friendly with everyone else. And neighborly toward him.

The sun felt hot on Nathan's back, the water streaming into the horse trough making him thirsty. Ethan was in the barn, puttering, killing time. Last Nathan knew, Marsh had been doing dishes and Zack was in the shower, making himself presentable to stand before the judge in Murdo. The night Nathan had picked him up and driven him home, Zack had spat out only a few words, but it had been enough to convey his intentions. He'd gotten himself into this mess and he would get himself out of it.

"That sun sure feels hot," Ethan said.

Watching the water level rise in the trough, Nathan nodded. Behind him Ethan climbed to the top of the fence and uncoiled a rope. "I'm thinking about going with Zack."

Just then Marsh stepped onto the porch. As he hobbled closer, Nathan saw that he was wearing clean clothes and a good cowboy boot on the foot not encased in a walking cast. Ethan looked pretty spiffed up, too.

Nathan turned off the water and exchanged looks with the other two Quinns. Last night he'd decided to go with Zack, assuming that either Marsh or Ethan could pick Holly up from her after-school job. It seemed they'd all had the same idea.

He was running through his options and considering alternate solutions when Zack stepped onto the porch. Seeing his three older brothers, boots shined, shirts pressed, gazes on him, he let the screen door bang shut behind him. "I thought I made it clear that I can do this alone."

Ethan shrugged. "All for one and one for all."

Zack was the first to look away, and Nathan was reminded of the first time his youngest brother had been thrown from a horse. It had to hurt like a son of a gun, but that little kid hadn't cried. Ten years younger than Nathan, Zack had worked so hard to keep up with his three older brothers. When he fell, he picked himself up and ran even faster to catch up. It wasn't always easy being the oldest. It couldn't be easy being the youngest, either.

"You don't clean up too bad," Ethan said.

Zack made a sound Nathan heard all the way across the driveway. Marsh hobbled closer, and Nathan and Ethan fell into step beside him.

"If I was the judge," Marsh declared, "I'd not only let you off easy, but I'd kiss you, too."

And Ethan said, "Aren't you glad he's not the judge?"

Even Zack had a hard time not grinning over that one. "You're really all going with me?"

Nathan was in the middle of nodding when he heard a car in the distance. He still had to make arrangements to have Holly picked up after work. Maybe he should put a call in to her school, leaving a message that she was to ride the bus home today. That would leave Meredith shorthanded in the store. That part-time job had been a godsend after Mary had died. It had given Holly something to do, someplace to be other than up in her room, sad and alone, something to think about, and be excited about, while time passed and her heart began to slowly heal.

The car in the distance came closer, pulling into Crystal's driveway. His neighbor was home. His neighborly neighbor.

He had an idea.

He started toward his truck. "Don't leave without me," he called through his open window. Zack's appointment was at three. Murdo was twenty-five minutes away. It was five minutes before two. They still had plenty of time.

"Where are you going?" Ethan called.

"To ask the neighbor for a favor."

If Nathan's truck hadn't sputtered to life when it did, he might have heard Marsh say, "So that's what they're calling it these days."

It took less than half a minute to reach the Mulberry place. He was in the process of raising his hand to knock when Crystal appeared at the door, a hammer in one hand, a painted wooden sign in the other.

"Nathan!" Classical music was playing in the background. "Hello. What are you doing here?"

"Ethan, Marsh and I decided to present the judge with a united front on Zack's behalf this afternoon."

"That sounds like a good idea."

She raised her eyebrows slightly, waiting for him to continue.

Recognizing the prod for what it was, he said, "I was wondering if you might be able to pick up Holly for me."

"Of course I will."

She stepped onto the porch with him, the ever-present breeze ruffling the baggy legs of her pale-green trousers, the heels of her shoes bringing her within a few inches of being eye-level with him. She looked feminine and soft, and she made him feel big and masculine and strong.

Nathan cleared his throat. "I'll compensate you for gasoline."

"That's what you think."

He did a double take.

And she smiled. "What are neighbors for? What time?"

"We have to be in Murdo by three."

"I meant what time is Holly getting out of work today?"

Nathan chastised himself. He would have known that, if he hadn't gotten sidetracked. He seemed to get sidetracked around her a lot. "Four-thirty." He glanced at the hammer in her hand. "What are you doing with that?"

She stepped around him, leaving behind the summery, musky scent of her perfume. "I was just getting ready to hang my shingle." She held up the sign, and Nathan recognized the work of Louetta Kincaid, the town's artist.

He reached for the hammer. "Where do you want it?"

"I thought you said you have to be in Murdo."

"I'd rather kill time here than cool my heels in the county courthouse. Besides, what are neighbors for?"

She pointed to the place directly over the steps. Positioning the sign over his head, he said, "Here?"

"A little to the right."

Nathan made short work of pounding in the nail and hanging the sign. Crystal stood back to admire her new shingle:

E. Crystal Galloway, LPC, Family Counselor.

The letters were elongated, the ends curling, forming a vine, which trailed all the way around the sign's perimeter. Louetta really had done a beautiful job.

"What does the E stand for?"

She looked up suddenly, and she remembered that Nathan hadn't stopped over these past several days the way the other Quinns had. He held himself more aloof. She didn't know if he was that way around everyone or only with her.

"Oh, no you don't. I've come to terms with the name my parents gave me. Using the initial is my way of acknowledging my past. It doesn't mean I like it."

"Come on. It can't be that bad."

Only someone whose name was Nathan could say something like that. Shrugging, she said, "I suppose I could tell you."

He waited expectantly.

And she said, "But then I'm afraid I'd have to kill you."

He cracked a smile. "You could probably enlist my daughter's help with that."

"Holly's angry with you, is she?"

"She's being completely unreasonable."

"I take it she told you about her opportunity to go to Boston."

"She came to you first?"

Crystal took a frank look at Nathan. He was good-looking, but there was nothing unusual about the cut of his dark hair or the angle of his chin. It wasn't unusual to see skin so tanned out here, and although his white shirt looked freshly ironed and his hat looked new, his attire was no different from dozens of other men's in this area. So it wasn't the clothing that made her feel so breathless.

"Holly mentioned it a few days ago." Assuming a professional stance, weight distributed on one foot, arms folded, chin raised, she said, "How does that make you feel?"

Nathan ran a finger between his neck and the collar of his shirt. Her attitude may have been no-nonsense, but her voice was sultry and deep, a slow sweep across his senses. Her green eyes appeared darker in the shadowy portion of the porch. He had a sudden image of how they might look beneath a moonlit sky, or in a room with no light at all.

He toyed with the idea of reaching a finger to her face and touching her cheek. Needing something else to do with his hands, he fumbled with his bolo tie. "What was your advice?" he asked.

"My advice?"

If felt good not to be the one not following the conversation for a change. "To Holly. When she told you about her 'opportunity of a lifetime.'"

She linked her fingers around the hammer and shrugged. "I told her to be open and honest. I take it you aren't going to let her go?"

"She would miss school."

"Could she make up the work?"

"That's not the point."

"What is the point?" Crystal asked.

"The point is, I don't think Boston is any place for an unchaperoned fifteen-year-old girl to be for two days, let alone an entire week. She insists I don't understand."

"Holly's only fifteen?" Crystal's hand went to the top button on her lightweight sweater. "She's an eleventh grader, isn't she?"

"She could read when she was only four. Mary and I decided to send her to school. It's always come easy to her, so easy that she even skipped a grade. That doesn't mean she should be traipsing off to large cities alone, no matter what kind of opportunity this is."

Nathan let his gaze stray to the rolling hills in the distance. The mulberry bushes obstructed the view of his own house, but farther to the east a herd of brown cattle lumbered across the horizon. Soon it would be roundup time. There would be branding to do and fences to mend and crops to tend and later harvest. They would need every pair of hands, including Zack's.

First, he had to help Zack out of the trouble he was in. Nathan had to get going. And he would. He glanced at his watch.

He would leave. In a minute.

"There are a thousand careers to choose from, and my daughter wants to be a concert violinist."

"Would you rather have her fascinated with music at this age, or fascinated with boys the way I was?"

"You liked boys, did you?"

A warm, delicious shudder started in that sensitive place at the base of Crystal's neck. It moved downward and outward and downward again, all the way to her fingers and toes. "Oh, yeah. I liked boys a lot."

"What about now?"

The wind blew a shock of her long, wavy hair into her eyes, blinding her. Crystal pushed the hair out of her eyes, tucking it behind her ear. It was broad daylight, and yet the air surrounding her and Nathan seemed hazy. Somehow, they'd turned, facing each other, her head tipped up, his down. The wind sighed through the eaves, brushing narrow branches against the house. Mozart's cheerful, vigorous music played on the old Victrola she'd discovered in the attic. It covered the quiet, but it didn't quiet the catch in her breathing.

"Do I like boys now?" she whispered, moistening her lips. "I guess you could say that now I can pretty much take them or leave them."

He eased closer. "Know what I think?"

No, she thought, she didn't know what he thought, but if he came any closer, she was going to know how he felt.

His gaze delved into hers. This close she could see her own reflection in his dark-brown eyes. This close she could breathe in his scent—the scent of soap, clean clothes and wide-open spaces.

"I think you like men, me in particular."

"Don't let it go to your head."

Heat charged through Nathan. He couldn't control where it was headed, but it most definitely didn't go to his head. "Would you tell me something, Crystal?"

She took her sweet time replying. "I'll try."

"I was just wondering…" He lowered his face by degrees, his mouth a hair's breadth from hers as he whispered, "How does this make you feel?"

Devilment danced in her eyes and a smile pulled at her mouth as she said, "If you put your money where your mouth is, cowboy, you might just find out."

The breath rushed out of him. He didn't put his money where his mouth was. Instead, he touched his mouth to hers.

Chapter Four

Crystal was fairly certain she'd been prepared for Nathan's kiss. She'd been wrong. Nothing could have prepared her for the sensation the joining of their mouths evoked. She'd once written a paper about kissing, for a psych class in college. She'd done extensive research on the subject of how and when and why humans kiss. Another time, she'd taken a different approach on the same subject, turning in an in-depth paper for a humanities class. She'd kissed a lot of boys, and later, a few men. Kissing Nathan Quinn was like starting from scratch.

His mouth moved over hers, his lips firm yet gentle, the kiss tentative as only a first kiss could be. It changed gradually, becoming exploratory, growing more intimate. It was heavenly, no doubt about it.

In some far corner of her mind she was aware that the Victrola had stopped playing in the living room. Without it the afternoon was silent, except for the breeze and the sound Nathan made deep in his throat.

His hands rested lightly on her waist, steadying her gently. He eased the tip of his boot between her feet, the action bringing their bodies just close enough that her breasts grazed his chest, and his knee touched her thigh. He groaned, moving his mouth across hers, deepening the kiss. Something went warm inside her, something far deeper than her sweater or the warm May afternoon. Her breathing became shallow, her pulse sped up, and her thoughts turned hazy.

She would never know how she managed to hold on to the hammer in her right hand. Her left hand glided up his arm, across his shoulder, resting lightly on the back of his neck. His body, muscular and warm, felt like a dream. But he was solid, strong, real.

Desire swirled between them, through them. And yet he didn't take the kiss any further, nor did she. It was far enough. It was perfect, the kiss of a man who could take a woman to incredible heights of passion while holding her secrets as safely as he was holding her right now. Until this moment she hadn't met a man with whom she might share her secrets. It was a dreamy notion, which was strange in itself, because Crystal wasn't normally given to dreaminess.

It took a moment for her to realize that the kiss was over and he'd drawn away. She opened her eyes, relieved and pleased that he appeared to be as dazed as she was.

Nathan took a deep breath and another step back. He'd lost his train of thought, his purpose for being here. For a moment he'd lost himself in Crystal's softness, in her scent, the wet, warm caress of her lips against his. Her eyes were dewy and deep. Staring into them, he couldn't think of anything to say.

Crystal winked.

In a whoosh it all came back to him—his reason for stopping by, his reason for needing to leave now. He adjusted his hat, shook his head. "I think that might have crossed the 'neighborly' line."

"You really think so?" She seemed to enjoy teasing him. "I haven't kissed anybody in a long time," she said, her fingers toying with that lightweight hammer, her eyes toying with him. "I guess it's like riding a bike."

"That was nothing like riding a bike."

Her smile grew. "Maybe you're right." She motioned to his truck. "Unless you want to have to try to explain to Marsh what took you so long, you might want to consider leaving now. Don't worry about Holly. I'll make sure she gets home."

The last thing Crystal expected Nathan to do was smile. It left her speechless, and that seldom happened to her.

She remained where she was on her porch, watching as he drove away. It occurred to her that she hadn't noticed his wedding ring today. That didn't mean he wasn't wearing it. She ran her tongue over her lips, remembering his kiss. She didn't know whether he was completely ready to move forward with his life, but that kiss had definitely been an encouraging step in the right direction.

Crystal was admiring the new filly with Holly when Nathan and his brothers returned from Murdo. She was too far away to tell how the meeting had gone. Zack was the first out of the extended-cab truck and the first to disappear inside the house. The door slammed, but that was nothing new. She'd noticed that they all let the old screen door bounce closed behind them. Although Marsh and Nathan followed more slowly, she couldn't be sure whether the judge had given them good news or bad. They, too, disappeared inside the house without a word.

Minutes later all four of them emerged. Crisp, clean hats exchanged for everyday ones, they all went in different directions. Marsh climbed into his truck and drove away, Zack strode to another outbuilding, and Ethan hopped in the Jeep and took off down a lane to God only knew where.

Nathan walked toward the corral. And Holly made noises about doing her homework. She glanced shyly at Crystal, made a halfhearted attempt at saying hello to her dad, then excused herself, thanking Crystal for the ride home at the same time.

Moments later the screen door banged closed.

A tense silence ensued. Since it could have been due to Holly, Zack, that kiss on Crystal's porch, or something else entirely, Crystal decided not to place too much emphasis on it.

The little horse whinnied, chasing after its mother, who apparently wasn't ready to feed her baby just yet. The filly was nothing if not persistent. It was comical, endearing, more entertaining than television. Hitching one foot on the lowest board, and resting her forearms on the top one, Crystal said, "Holly said you named the new filly Lucky."

He glanced at the seven stitches he'd gotten as a result of the horse's birth. "You said seven's lucky. Did she tell you she's still mad at me, too?"

Crystal shook her head. "I could see that for myself. That's the beauty of fifteen-year-old girls. You always know where you stand with them." Unlike their fathers. "I take it you haven't changed your mind about allowing her to go to Boston."

Nathan leaned tiredly on the gate. "Between Holly's silent treatment and Zack's sullenness, the place has felt like a morgue."

"Things didn't go well with the judge?"

"It wasn't as bad as it could have been. Zack has to pay a fine, do some community service. As if there isn't enough work to do on a ranch."

"What did Zack say about it?"

Nathan made a derogatory sound under his breath. "Zack doesn't say much about anything. Sometimes I swear Holly's taking lessons from him."

Little Lucky got her way on the other side of the corral, suckling to her hearts content. "Maybe this is more important to her than you realize, Nathan."

"I know how important it is to her, dammit." The mare

turned her head all the way around at the tone in his voice. Lowering the volume, Nathan said, "She's still too young. And Boston's too far."

"Maybe Holly is too young to go that far, for that long, by herself."

Finally, he thought, someone who understood.

"But somebody could go with her."

Acknowledging that his relief had probably been the shortest lived in history, he said, "I can't go. We've divided the herd. The next step is selling a portion. There are trucks coming, deals to make so we can eat next winter so I can pay for Holly's music lessons and send her to college, and maybe pay for her wedding someday, and everything she'll need between now and then."

She paused, as if to make sure he was finished. "Perhaps somebody else could go."

"Like who?"

She shrugged. "Someone who needs a change of scenery. Someone who needs a change of pace…"

He let his gaze stray to the rolling hills in the distance where the best beef cattle this ranch had seen in a decade were grazing on pastures that were still green from the winter snow and spring rain.

"…someone who hasn't been very happy lately," she added.

She could have been referring to any number of area bachelors. She could have been referring to him. His thoughts scrambled as if short-circuited. Was that what he was now? A bachelor?

His thumb automatically went to his wedding ring. No, he was a widower. There was a huge difference.

Alone was alone, the voice of his conscience—or was it his heart—whispered.

He turned his head slowly, studying Crystal's profile. From this angle she looked extremely intelligent, citified.

Beautiful. "Did you have someone in particular in mind?" he asked.

It was only when she looked directly at him that the imp inside her became apparent. Giving him a look only a woman could give a man, she said, "I was thinking of someone who needs to do something meaningful and worthwhile with his life, someone who might feel better about himself if he helped out his brother."

"Zack."

"That's a great idea!" Her green eyes twinkled.

"You think you're so smart."

She nudged him flirtily with her shoulder. "You're not so dumb yourself."

He grew silent, thinking. Finally, he said, "I suppose I could mention it to Zack. We should be done with branding by then. If I decide to let Holly go, I'll never hear the end of it. It's already Crystal this and Crystal that."

"Does that bother you?"

The wind fluttered her sweater, blowing wisps of hair off her face. "I passed bothered a week ago, Crystal." The very air he breathed was charged with energy that transferred into a physical awareness he wasn't sure what to do with. "Marsh accused me of acting like a bear with a sore paw."

"That's part of your charm."

"I thought you said Marsh was the charming one."

Staring into Nathan's dark-brown eyes, Crystal thought some psychiatric gibberish about birth order and sibling rivalry, but simply said, "Maybe it's an inherent Quinn trait."

He laughed suddenly, a deep, rumbling, masculine sound that made her heart flutter and her fingers still along the vee neckline of her sweater. The crash of metal falling on cement drew both their gazes toward the shed where Zack had disappeared a little while ago.

"I guess I should go talk to Zack about going to Boston with Holly while there are still tools and equipment left."

"Do you think he'll be receptive to the idea?" she asked.

Nathan shrugged. "Only one way to find out. I never would have thought I'd entrust my daughter to my hell-raising baby brother."

"You must believe he'd watch out for her."

"If I didn't think he'd die before he'd let anything happen to a hair on her head, I wouldn't even be considering it." He heaved a heavy sigh. "That girl's been the reason I get up every morning. What in God's name am I going to do while she's gone?"

There were two things Crystal noticed. The first was that it sounded as if Nathan had decided to allow Holly to go to Boston, providing Zack went with her. The second was that his gaze had gotten stuck below her shoulders.

"Something tells me," she said quietly, her own gaze falling to his mouth, "that you'll think of something."

Their eyes met, held. She was the first to find her voice. "I'll leave you to your brother."

She started to walk away.

"Crystal?"

She slowed, but didn't stop completely. "Yes?" she called over her shoulder.

"Thanks."

"You're welcome. Goodbye, Nathan."

Nathan watched her drive away. He would have liked to follow her. He couldn't seem to get her scent out of his nostrils, her laughter out of his head, her out of his system. He wanted to kiss her. Again. Until today he hadn't kissed another woman except Mary in, criminy, in forever. Crystal Galloway was a worldly woman. What on earth could an ordinary rancher have to offer a woman like her? It was a disquieting thought. Now, if someone would alert the rest of him, he might be able to do something about the little problem he was having getting her out of his mind.

Problems were nothing new to Nathan. It just so happened he was a firm believer in two surefire cures. Get busy. And stay that way.

With that in mind, he headed for the shed to talk to Zack.

The newspaper crinkled beneath Nathan's grip. Blinking, he gave up trying to concentrate on the political section and reached for the local news section. Five minutes later he blinked again. Unable to recall a word he'd read, he tossed the paper aside and stood.

Rain pelted the darkened windows, drenching the siding, soaking into the ground. It couldn't have come at a better time. They'd finished branding yesterday, just under the wire for Zack to go to Boston with Holly. There was no thunder or lightning. It was just what they needed. It was perfect.

He wished it would stop.

Holly and Zack had left that morning. Nathan, Marsh and Ethan had all seen them off at the airport in Pierre. Holly had called home two hours ago to let Nathan know they'd arrived safely. For a girl who insisted the trip had been uneventful so far, her voice had been full of excitement. Zack had come on the line, sputtering that so far, he'd only had to break one guy's nose and two men's arms for looking at Holly. "But don't worry," he'd laughed. "It's early."

Marsh and Ethan had found it a lot funnier than Nathan had. The two middle Quinns agreed that if they didn't know him, they wouldn't mess with the likes of Zack Quinn.

Holly was in good hands.

Nathan wandered out to the kitchen, thinking that maybe he should have taken Marsh and Ethan up on their invitation to head down to Cedar Butte with them, looking for a little action. Truth was, Nathan wouldn't have known what to do with any action if he'd found it.

He walked around the old pine table, wandered out to

the sunporch and came in again. He knew the house like the back of his hand. He and his brothers had been raised in this house, and their father before them. His dad had died fifteen years ago, his mother two years later. His memories of them had grown hazy around the edges the way memories often did. Now his sweet Mary was buried right next to them. He tried to picture her in this very kitchen. He smiled, because that was the way he remembered her most often, cooking, humming and smiling. Now and then he got an image of the way she'd been near the end, her beautiful auburn hair gone, her face so pale, her hands, once so strong and nurturing, weak, her skin so thin it was almost transparent. Even those memories were growing hazy around the edges, as if taken with a camera slightly out of focus.

It had only been a year, for crying out loud. Fifteen months, that annoying voice of reason reminded him. Three years since she was truly healthy.

One year was a long time. Sometimes, three years felt like forever.

He was getting maudlin. The rain made everything gloomy. And it was too quiet here. Yep, he should have gone looking for a little excitement with Marsh and Ethan. Forget what he'd told them, that there was plenty of excitement right here. He looked at the piles of dirty jeans and shirts on the floor in the laundry room. He'd drawn laundry duty this week. A dismal job anytime. Downright depressing tonight.

What else could he do?

What did anyone do in Jasper Gulch? He and Mary used to get ice-cream sundaes at Mel's diner once in a while. More often than not, they'd catch a movie in Pierre, or take Holly roller-skating in Murdo. Life had been so easy back then. Mary had taken care of the fun. She'd taken care of a lot of things. Now she was gone.

Holly was, too. But she wasn't gone forever. She would be back in a week.

This time.

What about next year, and the year after? What would he do then?

He was getting maudlin again.

It was too quiet here. He switched on the radio. And too dark. He switched on the light.

He paced from one end of the first floor to the other. Great. Now he was alone in a noisy, bright house. Alone was alone.

He wound up in the bathroom, staring at his reflection. He needed a shave. He needed a change of scenery, where there was real noise made by real people. Where would he find that?

He peered out the rain-streaked window over the old cast-iron tub. There was a place like that right in Jasper Gulch.

He reached for his razor. It was Friday night. Hot dang. Nathan was going to town.

"It's up to you, Nathan. What's it gonna be?"

Nathan eyed his cards and then the five other people sitting around the table. Cletus McCully was puffing on a smelly cigar, the smoke rising like fog in the dimly lit room. Nathan had wanted noise. Noise was what he'd gotten. Somebody had produced the demo CD the Anderson brothers had sent. The Dakotas, formerly known as Neil, Ned and Norbert Anderson, three brothers from Jasper Gulch who'd left town last winter to play their music in Nashville, hadn't sounded half-bad the first time or two he'd heard their CD. Some of the local boys had started to complain when they'd heard the same song four and five times in a row.

Boomer Brown, co-owner of the place, had fired up the mechanical bull, then proceeded to stage a competition to see who could ride the thing the longest and the fastest. Nathan had considered taking a turn. Instead, he'd taken Forest's place at the poker table.

Now Nathan studied the competition. Hal and Roy Everts, two of Cletus McCully's cronies, had tossed in their cards a while ago. That had left Cletus McCully and Doc Masey on the other side of the table, and Crystal and Nathan on this side. The only woman in the place besides the owner, Crystal seemed right at home. She laughed often, shuffled the cards like a pro, cracked a joke of her own from time to time and still managed to behave like a lady.

Her green eyes were wide open right now, her smile artful and serene. Maybe it was a poker face. Maybe not. It cut Nathan off at the knees either way. It made him feel young. Or maybe being in the Crazy Horse on a Friday night was responsible for that.

"Well, boy?" Cletus prodded around the cigar clamped tight between his teeth.

No. That wasn't what was making him feel young. Crystal was responsible for that. That could be a dangerous thing. He threw in his cards. "I'd better quit before I lose the ranch."

"Doc?" Cletus said.

Doc grumbled, "If I have to listen to that song one more time, I'm going to jump off a bridge." He glared at his cards. "Aw, hell, I fold."

"Looks like it's just me and you, little lady," Cletus called. "Hey, DoraLee, would ya bring us another round?"

Crystal studied the cards in her hand. She'd won the first four games in a row. As a result, she'd had an impressive stack of matchsticks in front of her. She'd lost the last two games.

"What's the matter, girl?" that old coot Cletus said, his voice as snappy as his suspenders. "Somethin' happen to your concentration?"

Crystal knew what Cletus was doing. He was trying to

needle her. Cletus liked to win. Forget that she'd seen him deal from the bottom of the deck. Forget that he was right about the fact that she'd been having a teensy bit of trouble concentrating these last two games.

Ever since Nathan had joined them.

She studied the three tens in her hand, and the pair of fours right next to them. Then she studied Cletus. Someone had once told her he was in his early eighties. She would have guessed older. His face was deeply lined; his eyes were bright with mischief. He'd buried his son and daughter-in-law years ago and had raised his grandson and granddaughter. These days he spent a good deal of his daylight hours on the bench in front of the post office. From what Crystal could tell, he'd always spent a good share of his evening hours right here at the Crazy Horse, swapping stories and playing cards.

Those mischievous eyes of his were practically dancing right now. She had no idea if his cards were really as good as he wanted her to believe they were. She wondered if they could beat a full house.

She laid her cards facedown in front of her. Strumming her fingers, she glanced at the other men around the table. They were all looking at her expectantly. Nathan was the only one she had trouble looking away from.

She hadn't seen or heard from him since the week before, when he'd talked to her out by the corral. Oh, she'd heard about him from Marsh, Ethan and Zack. It seemed they'd all spent most of the week out on the range, rounding up cattle and then branding the yearlings, a barbaric practice if there ever was one. Crystal tried really hard not to imagine those hands wielding a branding iron. It was even more difficult not to imagine them warm and strong on her body. Perhaps that was the reason she forced her gaze away every time she caught herself staring at those scraped knuckles and blunt-tipped fingers. Or, it could have had something to do with the fact that he still wore his wedding ring.

Cletus must have noticed how valiantly Crystal was trying not to look at Nathan's hands, and how miserably she was failing, because the next time she looked at the old codger, his eyes were far too knowing. "Well?" he prodded.

She sighed. And he looked victorious for a moment. Until she tossed in three matchsticks. "I call."

His eyes widened beneath his bushy white brows. Beside her, Nathan chuckled. "She's no pushover, is she Cletus?"

Cletus laid down his cards, grumbling under his breath. Crystal glanced at his three fives and pair of sevens, then turned her bigger, better full house over for him to see.

"She beat you fair and square, old man," Doc exclaimed.

"Who're you callin' old?"

Everybody knew that Cletus didn't give a lick about being called old. He was just sore about losing. Luckily, DoraLee Brown brought the next round of drinks right then.

"Ready to play another one?" Hal Everts asked.

Crystal shook her head and pushed back her chair. Nathan was suddenly there, pulling it out for her. She slid off the other side and slowly stood. Their eyes met. All at once the entire room went quiet. Surely it was a coincidence that the mechanical bull stopped right then and the demo CD ended. There was nothing coincidental about all the eyes on them, though.

"Anybody have any quarters?" she asked.

Nathan fished a few out of his pocket.

Crystal took them from him and marched to the other side of the room where she promptly fed them into the jukebox. Seconds after punching a button, a twangy tune filled the air.

"I didn't know you were a Hank Williams fan," Forest said from a nearby table.

"Who? Oh. Yes. Right."

It was eleven o'clock. She made her way toward the back

where she'd left her purse. "I suppose it's still raining cats and dogs out there," she said to no one in particular.

"You fixin' to leave?" Forest called.

She nodded.

"But you haven't even listened to the song you just chose!"

What could she say? So she shrugged and smiled.

"Where are you parked?" Nathan asked.

"Down the street a ways." She cast a glance around the table. "Good night, everybody."

"Bye."

"See ya later."

"Yeah, so long, Crystal."

She didn't know Nathan was right behind her until he snagged his cowboy hat off the peg on the hat rack by the door where she'd left her umbrella. "Are you leaving, too?" she asked.

His eyes were steady as he said, "As soon as I walk you to your car."

Behind them, the jukebox played on, covering the clink of glass and the low rumble of voices. "Folks are going to talk if you do that, Nathan. They're going to raise their eyebrows and wonder out loud about Nathan Quinn and that Galloway woman."

He adjusted his hat and reached for the door. "They're already wondering that. A few bets have been placed, dollar bills have been exchanged."

Crystal digested the information as they walked out into the dark, rainy night. She opened her big, polka-dot umbrella, and held it to one side so it covered his head, too.

Neither of them spoke while they walked to her car. Fishing her keys out of her purse, she aimed the control at the door and pushed the remote, unlocking her door. "That was extremely gentlemanly of you," she said. "But I know self-defense, Nathan."

"What would you say if I told you I didn't do it to protect you, and I'm not feeling terribly gentlemanly?"

Rain pelted the umbrella, echoing around their ears. "I'd say good for you and thanks just the same."

Their faces were close. Although it was too dark to see his expression, she sensed his smile. An answering one found its way to her lips. She thought about how he'd kissed her, and how much time he was taking before doing it again. He was an honorable man who didn't take commitment lightly, a man who would be worth the wait to a woman willing to take the risk. Was she that woman? The thought came, unbidden.

There was always a risk when hearts were involved. She knew that painfully well.

He opened her door and she lowered the umbrella. Reaching up on tiptoe, she kissed his cheek. "I think you're a rarity in this day and age, a perfect, patient gentleman in the true sense of the word."

With the press of a button, her umbrella folded. Her door clicked shut, and the engine started.

Nathan didn't move until after she drove away.

The rain ran in little rivers down his hat, splashing in the puddles at his feet. With three fingers he covered the cheek Crystal had just kissed. His pulse had leaped when she'd done that. It was erratic even now.

She thought he was patient? A sense of guilt from long ago washed over him. He hadn't always been patient. In fact, his impatience had led to the greatest sadness of Mary's life. She'd never blamed him, but he'd blamed himself.

He'd made her happy, hadn't he?

Yes, he knew he had. She'd told him often. Now she was gone. He'd buried her in a beautiful casket on a yellow pillow, her favorite color. In doing so, he'd buried the only other person who'd known of the guilt he carried, the only other person who knew he wasn't perfect at all.

* * *

Crystal heard the putt and growl and the occasional back-fire of a motorcycle in the distance, but she didn't pay much attention until it pulled into her driveway and crawled to a stop a dozen feet from the area where she was planting petunias. Feeling a little awestruck at the sight of Nathan on a motorcycle, she went up to her knees. His hair was windblown, his expression unreadable. On a horse he looked every bit a rancher. On a motorcycle he looked more like a rascal or a rogue.

"I don't believe I've ever seen you out without your hat," she said loud enough for him to hear over the engine noise.

Nathan's mouth opened, but no sound came out. With a shake of his head, he faced the fact that he never knew what Crystal was going to do or say. There was one thing he wanted her to know.

"I'm not perfect. Last night you hinted that I was. I have a temper. And as far as patience goes, Mary used to say it was a good thing I didn't want to be a doctor, because it took patients to be one of those."

She graced him with a slow, sexy smile, then peeled her gardening gloves off, one finger at a time. Dropping them to the cloth she'd been kneeling on, she rose to her feet. Her jeans had a tear in one knee, the fabric so faded and worn they were nearly white. They hugged her hips and thighs, much the way her pale-green T-shirt hugged the curves slightly higher.

By the time his gaze made it all the way to her face, she wavered him a woman-soft smile that felt like a kick in his gut. But a little lower, now that was another story.

He'd spent the better part of the morning and half the afternoon getting his old motorcycle running. He hadn't wasted that much time on something not related to work in years. Since he'd been young. Initially he'd tackled it be-cause he'd thought puttering would alleviate his pent-up energy. The engine wasn't the only thing that had backfired. Revving up the engine had revved him up. Dang. He'd felt like a kid again.

Forget how dangerous feeling like that could be. He'd wanted to take the cycle for a ride.

He'd put the bike on the kickstand, strode into the house and washed up. He'd stared at his clean-scrubbed hands, thinking how good it was to have those blasted stitches out. He'd turned his left hand over, staring at the ring.

Before he could analyze his actions, he'd marched into his bedroom. When he'd emerged, his blood had been chugging through his veins. He'd left his cowboy hat on the peg by the door, and returned to the motorcycle. Seconds later he'd been buzzing through the yard, around the barns, down the driveway.

He wasn't surprised he'd ended up here. It seemed he always gravitated toward Crystal these days. It wasn't something he chose, and yet there seemed to be no use resisting. Since he'd met her, just being in the same county with her sent anticipation and a heady sense of urgency racing through him. It didn't feel good, exactly. It didn't feel bad, exactly, either. What it felt was damn confusing.

He knew the exact moment she noticed that he was missing more than his hat. Her green eyes widened, and her lips parted.

"I took it off five minutes ago," he said, his thumb automatically going to his ringless left hand. "I'm feeling naked without it. Do you want to go for a ride on my motorcycle with me or don't you?"

Her grin was slow and thoughtful, contagious, sexy as hell. "A naked man on a motorcycle. How on earth could I pass that up?"

He stood up to give her room. She swung a long, luscious leg over the seat and scooted back a little. There was a moment of hesitation. But only one. And then her arms glided around his waist. Nathan's stomach muscles clenched, relaxed, clenched again as she pressed her warm, soft curves into his back.

Easy, he told himself. And he gave the motorcycle a little gas.

Chapter Five

"Do you mind if we stop here?" Crystal called into Nathan's ear, pointing to an area on their left.

Nathan slowed the motorcycle to a crawl. Mind? A warm wind at his face, a warm woman at his back, he could have gone on riding for miles.

He'd taken the trail that meandered toward the southern boundary of the Quinn ranch. Coming to a complete stop, he braced the bike with his feet. Twenty or thirty feet beyond the edge of the trail, the land dropped off into a shallow gully. "Are you sure you want to stop here?"

Crystal scooted backward, then stood, swinging one leg over the back of the seat. "Where are we?"

He cut the engine. Propping the motorcycle on its stand, he joined her on a seldom-used path. "We call it the Quinn badlands. This land isn't really as barren as the state's most infamous badlands southeast of the Black Hills, but it's too craggy, rocky and unlevel to grow crops or graze cattle. Luckily, there are only a few areas like this on our property. We're only a mile from the creek. I took this route because it's on higher ground, and after last night's rain..."

"It's beautiful."

Nathan stared, first at her and then at the land around them. Wind and water had eroded the soil, pitting the exposed rock and cutting sharp crevices into the sloping hills. Beautiful? "Aside from scrub bushes and prairie grass, nothing grows here. The soil is unworkable, worthless to ranchers, farmers, developers, you name it."

Just then, a pheasant called out to its mate. "It isn't worthless to all creatures," she said quietly. "Why, it's places like this that are quintessential to a host of wildlife. Not to mention works of art. It's nature's sculpture. Well, except for that pile of rubbish over there."

Leave it to a city girl to find beauty in a desolate place like this. He fell into step beside her, picking his way down the sloping, unlevel ground. "My parents and grandparents used it for a junk heap. Of course, that was before anyone had heard of recycling."

"Certain segments of our society would treat a person with complete and utter disdain for that. Come on. I'll bet there are all kinds of treasures in that pile."

They crunched over one broken or rotting treasure after another. Stepping around a small, rusty bicycle, she said, "Was that yours?"

Nathan shook his head. "It was Ethan's first bike, bent beyond repair after our dad backed over it early one morning. I was always more interested in the gasoline-powered variety."

They sidestepped an assortment of rusty horseshoes, what probably amounted to a truckload of glass bottles, a broken wooden barrel and a cracked enamel sink. "Then you've had motorcycles for a long time?" she asked.

"I used to. When I was young."

"What do you consider young?" She bent down. "Look."

Nathan was growing accustomed to the way she went

from one topic to another. He was also growing accustomed to her unique outlook on life.

Hidden from view by a scraggly bush on the edge of tall prairie grass and a rotting wooden bucket was a nest. "A bobwhite's?" she asked.

He leaned closer, getting a good look at the speckled eggs. "A horned lark. And for your information I'm feeling younger all the time."

Their heads were bent close, her face slightly lower than his. "Why do you suppose that is?"

Her eyelashes cast shadows beneath her eyes when she blinked, her skin golden in the late-afternoon light. His gaze strayed to her mouth and stayed there. "Are you playing counselor, Crystal?"

The tease smiled. And his blood heated.

Her hair was mussed from the ride here, the tresses a mass of tangled waves that tugged at a man's imagination. She wore faded jeans and a sleeveless white shirt, normal female attire. Except she wasn't like most women he knew. She used words like *perhaps* and *disdain, rubbish* and *quintessential,* proper words for a woman whose kiss knocked a man's socks off.

"I bet you drove the boys crazy in school."

"Am I driving you crazy, Nathan?"

He had to remind himself to breathe. "You're driving me to distraction and you know it."

Just then a bird twittered. "Hear that?" she asked.

"A quail."

"Are you sure? I've been studying birdcalls. I believe that was a partridge. The tone is just slightly different than a quail's, isn't it?"

He shrugged. "You have an ear for music, for pitch and tone. Holly's like that, too."

"And you're not?"

He shook his head, his gaze still on her mouth. "I'm more of a hands-on learner."

For a moment Crystal lost her train of thought. Her breathing became shallow, her pulse sped up, and her thoughts turned as hazy as a long-forgotten dream. She'd flirted with other men, years ago. Something told her that this was brand-new for Nathan.

"Did Holly get her musical talent from her mother, then?"

He shrugged. "I don't know where her talents came from. That girl's smarter than all of us."

Crystal was adept at reading between the lines, at deciphering facial expression and speech patterns. There was something about Nathan's answer, something in his expression and the halting words he'd used. "What do you mean?"

"About what?"

"About Holly and her musical talent." She noticed he was looking at her, but he didn't seem to be listening. "I saw her carrying a violin case one day. I never learned to play that particular instrument. It probably had something to do with the fact that my mother wanted me to, and don't tell anyone but I used to be slightly belligerent. If she and my father couldn't like me for myself, I wasn't going to be the prodigy they wanted me to be. Talk about cutting my nose off to spite my face. Of course, it took months of therapy before I realized that's what I had been doing."

"Crystal?"

"Yes?"

"I like your nose."

She blinked. "You do? Oh, well, I wasn't really fishing for a compliment, I was only trying to—"

"Crystal?"

Again she said, "Yes?"

"I was just wondering if you would mind if we stopped talking now."

Her gaze flew to his. There was no reproach in those dark, insolent, brown eyes of his, but there was a lazily seductive gleam that reminded her of how he'd looked when he'd first pulled into her driveway on that old motorcycle, all windblown hair and cowboy brawn.

"What would *we* do," she whispered, "if *we* didn't talk?"

"I have an idea."

He slid a hand into her hair, his fingers warm on her scalp.

He tilted her head, steadying it there. A partridge trilled. Or maybe Nathan was right and it was a quail. She was too busy closing her eyes dreamily to pay attention to anything not within inches of her, too busy swaying slightly, her lips parting as he covered them with his.

The first time he'd kissed her, he'd taken it slow. This kiss was different. This was more urgent, more knee weakening, toe curling, mind-boggling. It was the kiss of a man who knew what he wanted. He wanted her. Being wanted by Nathan Quinn was a heady sensation.

His hand slid out of her hair, down her neck, around her back, bringing her body against his. He groaned, deep in his throat. An answering sound found its way out of her mouth. The first time he'd kissed her, she'd been holding on to a hammer. This time she had nothing in her hand, so she filled her hands with him, with sinew and muscle and a soft, chambray shirt that bunched between her fingers.

He was like a man dying of thirst. And she was a mountain stream. She flowed over him, and his hands flowed over her, kneading, skimming, inching around her sides, covering her breasts. His fingers squeezed, caressed and cajoled, sending desire pouring through her, hot and heavy.

The kiss broke, and her head tipped back, a moan rising in her throat, the sun dancing on the other side of her closed lids. She thought he might lower his head and press his face where his hands had been. But something changed. It was as if he came to his senses. He stopped caressing. Stopped moving. Stopped breathing.

She straightened slowly. Opening her eyes, she stepped away and rearranged her clothes. He probably hadn't kissed another woman, let alone touched one so intimately, since his wife had died. Putting a little distance between them, she gave him a moment to get his feet back underneath him. The best way to do that was to talk.

And that's what she did. She talked about inconsequential things, like the weather, and how it differed in Philadelphia, where she was born and a host of other useless information. At one point he started listening. She knew, because he said, "I thought you said you were from Albuquerque."

Starting back the way they'd come, she said, "I've lived in a lot of places, and Albuquerque was one of them. But I was born in Philadelphia. My mother and father liked the culture there."

"And you didn't?"

"If you're looking, you can find culture almost anywhere."

"Where are you going?"

She cast a quick glance over her shoulder and called, "Back to the motorcycle. Isn't that what you wanted to do?"

Truthfully? Nathan thought. Hell, no, it wasn't what he wanted to do. What he wanted to do was go back to that gully, back to that kiss, and start again. He wanted to touch her again, to roll her underneath him and feel the entire length of her pressed along the entire length of him. That wasn't all he wanted.

When they reached the path, they were panting slightly from the uphill climb. That didn't stop Crystal from talking. "I hope you won't waste a lot of time agonizing over what just happened, Nathan. What you're feeling is normal."

"What am I feeling?" If she'd been looking, she would have noticed the change that came over him. Evidently, she was too busy psychoanalyzing him to do anything as mundane as look at him.

"It seems to me that those vows people take, 'till death do you part,' are much more pat for the partner who's gone," she said.

A dozen feet away, his motorcycle waited to give them a return ride home. Nathan reached it ahead of Crystal, his movements brisk, his fingers flexing in his effort to keep them from curling into fists. There wasn't much he could do about the cold note of sarcasm that crept into his voices as he said, "I think I know what your initial stands for."

"What?"

"Einstein."

Crystal's lips formed around a one-word question, but the single syllable didn't make it out of her mouth. She felt a tightening in her throat, and an ache slightly lower. Einstein. She'd been called worse things, some vulgar, some simply intended to bring her down a notch or two. But none had ever come out of the blue quite like Nathan's had.

She felt small, suddenly, like a shy animal face-to-face with a hunter ten times its size. In that moment she had a revelation. Nathan Quinn had the power to hurt her. Why he would want to was a mystery.

It wasn't a new phenomenon. She'd been hurt before, but it had been a while since she'd allowed anyone close enough to have that kind of power.

Finding her voice, she said, "The *E* doesn't stand for Einstein. I suppose I should be thankful for small favors."

Even to herself, her voice had sounded small. Nathan looked ill at ease suddenly.

He rocked the motorcycle from its kickstand and started the engine. Crystal climbed on behind him.

The return trip seemed to take forever. Perhaps that was because it was accomplished in total silence. She didn't wrap her arms around him as she had earlier. Instead, she clutched only his shirt. Holding herself stiffly away from him, she prayed she didn't fall off.

Twenty harrowing minutes later her house came into view. Relief washed over her. She kept a stiff upper lip as she climbed off the machine. She kept a firm resolve as she started for the wilting petunias she'd left out in the sun when Nathan had driven up and snapped his fingers. Good manners dictated that she thank him for the ride and bid him farewell. As far as she was concerned, good manners and Nathan Quinn could go straight to the same place.

It was quiet, Nathan thought. Too quiet.

It was past supper time, but hunger wasn't responsible for the knot in his stomach. He felt like hell, and he wasn't even sure why.

Crystal walked away from him, the epitome of affronted female pride. Her shoulders were back, her chin lifted, her backbone ramrod straight. He could have lived with her anger. But she didn't look angry. She looked, oh, hell. He'd hurt her.

He bit back a curse.

He turned the motorcycle off. And waited. She had to look at him sooner or later, didn't she?

Evidently not.

The only place she looked was at the soil she was digging in. He balanced the bike on the kickstand again and got off.

He strode to the edge of the flower bed near the porch step. She dug a hole. He planted his feet. She placed a plant in the hole. Then dug another. Surely, it was an accident that dirt landed on his boot. Like hell.

Finally, she said, "If you have something to say, you might as well say it."

He glanced at his watch, and then at the flat of flowers still waiting. Tamping the dirt off his boot, he said, "That quip about Einstein. I'd take it back if I could."

She went perfectly still for a moment. And then she said, "I've been called worse things."

"Not by me. I'm not perfect, but I'm rarely mean. I was angry. That's no excuse, I know."

She looked up at him. Shading her eyes with one hand, she said, "Why were you angry?"

"Because I'd just kissed you. I was trying to get myself under control. No matter how young I feel these days, I should be old enough to control my lust, to keep from copping a feel like some rutting teenager. If I felt guilty about anything, it was that. I didn't appreciate being analyzed."

Slowly she found her feet. Rubbing the dirt from her hands, she shrugged so gosh-darned sweetly his throat went dry. In a voice more kind than he deserved, she said, "I guess I'm like the orthodontist who's so busy noticing even the most minutely crooked tooth he misses the smile. I sensed your guilt. I was off the mark about the reason."

"I'd feel better if you were ticked. You should be fuming."

"You want me to demand retribution? I guess I could give you forty lashes."

He found himself smiling. "That sounds harsh."

The woman had class, finesse and a sense of humor. And breasts soft and lush enough to make a man forget his own name. He swallowed. Hard. "I'd better be going. It's my night to cook."

"I could make dinner, Nathan, thereby killing two birds with one stone. Now, where did I put that saltpeter?"

She seemed to enjoy his struggle to hide his surprise. "Saltpeter?"

She nodded smugly. "Potassium nitrate. Primarily it's used to make matches and explosives, but it was once thought to have, shall we say, the opposite effect of aphrodisiacs."

Forty lashes weren't that many. "Where do you keep your whip?" he asked.

Her throaty laughter reminded him that his body hadn't fully recovered from that little episode in the badlands. He didn't know what was happening to him. Oh, he knew what was happening, physically. But there was more to this than physical awareness.

"Are you considering my dinner invitation, Nathan?"

"First of all, it's called supper out here. Ethan and Marsh are counting on me to rustle up something for all of us."

"I'll tell you what," she said. "You go on home, and I'll throw enough food together for all of us. I have a refrigerator full of it. It'll take me half an hour or so to heat everything up. Think you can wait that long?"

"Waiting has never been my strong suit."

His gaze trailed down Crystal's body, causing her to doubt that he was referring to dinner. Several replies came to mind. Forfeiting all of them, she turned toward the porch steps.

"Crystal?"

She stopped on the top one.

"You don't really have any saltpeter, do you?"

She winked. "That's for me to know and you to find out."

She was already in the kitchen when she heard his motorcycle sputter to life. Her smile lasted long after the sound trailed away.

"Is that how you broke your ankle, then?" Crystal asked Marsh. "Jumping out of an airplane?"

"The jump went fine," Marsh said, spearing a green bean with his fork.

"It was the landing that got him," Nathan and Ethan said in unison.

Marsh shot his brothers a dagger, each, but it was Nathan he raised his eyebrows at. "Glad to see you're finally joining the conversation, even if your dazzling wit is at my expense."

Nathan and Ethan shared a chuckle. And then Nathan glanced at his watch. He'd done it often enough to make Crystal notice.

The table had been set on the screened sunporch when she'd arrived. Tonight was the first time she'd been inside the Quinn house. And while she hadn't actually had a tour, she'd gotten a hazy impression of a lot of rooms with scuffed hardwood floors and quaint, painted furniture. The living room had a stone fireplace. She'd caught a glimpse of a parlor that held an old, upright piano, the top literally covered with framed photographs. The kitchen was old, too, the stove one people from the city would pay a small fortune to own today. For all its charm, the room was sorely lacking in the gadget department. Luckily, what she couldn't find in the drawers, one of the Quinn brothers improvised.

She'd wondered how four grown men managed in one house. From what she could tell, they managed quite well. Still, she would have been hard-pressed to say who looked more dubious when she'd ladled the soup into bowls.

"It's borscht," she'd told them all.

"Are those beets in there?" Ethan had asked.

"Be thankful she left the saltpeter out," Nathan had said. But she'd noticed he'd waited for her to take the first taste.

Ethan had been amazed at the food she'd had stashed in her refrigerator. She'd half expected one of them to comment when she'd informed them that sometimes, late at night, she liked to cook. Surprisingly, no snide comments were forthcoming.

Nathan had grown quiet as the meal had progressed. Ethan must have noticed the furtive glances she was giving the brothers, because he said, "Do you have us figured out yet?"

She pulled a face. "I've already been accused of being analytical once today." She smiled broadly. "All right. If you insist. It's fairly obvious that Zack's the rebel of the family. And you, Ethan, are the peacemaker. You're all rugged, strong. Somebody taught you manners. You use the right fork, sit up straight, don't slurp your soup or talk with your mouths full.''

Marsh scratched his chest. Ethan pounded on his. Nathan and Crystal chuckled. His gaze met hers, and their laughter dwindled to smiles that were even more heartwarming.

"What about me?" he said.

"Nathan's the trustworthy, dependable one," Ethan answered for her.

Crystal thought there was more to him than that. Actually, there was more to all of them. Separately the brothers looked startlingly alike. Side by side their differences became more apparent. Nathan's hair was darker than the others. Ethan's mouth was wider, Marsh's eyebrows straighter, his eyes beneath them more deeply set. She would have been hard-pressed to say who was the most handsome. And yet her eyes were repeatedly drawn to Nathan's.

"I guess that leaves me," Marsh said.

Crystal had been so lost in Nathan, she'd forgotten they weren't alone. Turning to Marsh, she said, "I think you're a little of each of those things."

"A trustworthy, peacemaking rebel." Marsh wiggled his eyebrows. "How do you women resist me?"

"It's a chore, believe me. Is that why you don't live in Jasper Gulch? Because there weren't enough women to go around?"

Three pairs of brown eyes were suddenly downcast, and the room, all at once, was perfectly quiet. Marsh recovered first. "This house wasn't big enough for all of us."

Ethan's voice was unusually quiet as he said, "You love this land as much as we do, Marsh. You could have lived in Hester's place."

Another silence ensued. What in the world had Crystal stumbled upon?

Marsh and Nathan exchanged a look. Crystal didn't understand it, but there was something they weren't saying, something not even Ethan seemed to know for sure.

"Hester's house is pink," Marsh said.

Ethan jumped in. "That's true. Men can't live in pink houses."

Nodding, Marsh smiled at Crystal, and for the first time she noticed a dimple in one lean cheek. "Anyone care for more brioche?" he asked.

"More what?" Ethan asked.

"It's bread," Marsh answered. Shrugging at his brothers, he said, "I once dated a French girl. The language rubbed off."

"Yeah?" Ethan quipped. "In the eleventh grade, I French-kissed the prom queen—a senior, Suzie Baker."

"Suzie Baker," Marsh said. "I don't remember her."

"She was a petite redhead. Left right after graduation. She sure could kiss."

Crystal laughed in spite of herself. Nathan looked at his watch again.

"Is something wrong?" she asked.

He shrugged. "Holly hasn't called."

"That's right," Ethan said. "She hasn't."

During the lull that followed Crystal said, "Would any of you care for dessert?"

"You brought dessert, too?" Marsh asked.

"Can I pronounce it?" Ethan said at the same time.

Crystal smiled. "Can you pronounce crème brûlée?"

Crystal thought she heard Ethan mutter something about chocolate chip cookies, but he ate every last dollop of his dessert. The phone rang just as they were finishing. Nathan excused himself to answer it, and since Ethan was in charge of cleanup, Crystal accepted Marsh's invitation to take a walk with him out to the corral.

Actually, she walked. He hobbled.

It was that quiet time of the day, an hour before sunset,

when the blue was slipping from the sky and the sun's rays were turning the edges of the clouds gold and lavender. Bees buzzed, flies bothered the horses, causing them to swish their long tails.

"It's pretty here," she said. "Is it good to be back?"

"It's always good to come home."

She found herself wanting to understand the ties that bound these brothers as well as whatever had fragmented a few of them.

"Your mother must have been a proud woman."

"She was a spitfire. Didn't weigh more than 110 pounds, but that didn't stop her from chasing us around with a wooden spoon. Usually caught us, too."

"What about your father?"

"He didn't run as fast. I don't think he wanted to get away."

The horses turned at the sound of Crystal's throaty chuckle. "Did she and Mary get along?"

"Sure." He stared straight ahead. "I guess."

"You don't want to talk about Mary?"

"Honey, I'd rather talk about me."

Nathan was carrying in the last of the dishes when Crystal's and Marsh's laughter carried to his ears. Up to his forearms in dishwater, Ethan gestured with his head for Nathan to have a look out the window. "She sure is pretty," Ethan said.

Nathan didn't reply.

"I take it that wasn't Holly on the phone?"

This time Nathan scowled. "No."

Outside, Crystal laughed again, the sound seeping into Nathan's ears, shimmering into his thoughts. Ethan rinsed a pan. "You'd better put dibs on her if you want her."

Nathan felt his eyes narrow. "Dibs?"

"Yeah, you know. Stake your claim."

"We're not cavemen for God's sake.... Maybe I should speak for myself."

One part of Nathan's mind was aware of the water that sloshed to the floor as Ethan spun around. The next thing he knew, Ethan was behind him, trying to get him in a headlock. Nathan gave him a good jab with his elbow. Ethan returned the favor. They traipsed across the kitchen, rattling pots and pans and bumping into appliances.

The screen door opened on the other side of the room, the scrape of Marsh's cast as it slid across the floor mingling with thuds and oomphs.

"Oh, my gosh!" Crystal exclaimed. "What are you doing?"

"Nathan's itching for a fight. Oooh, ugh. And I'm giving it to him."

Suddenly Nathan slammed Ethan against the refrigerator. An instant later Ethan hauled Nathan around and shoved him against the wall.

"Marsh!" Crystal exclaimed. "Do something."

Marsh strode to the sink and ran himself a glass of water. "Who was on the phone?"

"Somebody trying to, oomph—" Nathan doubled over "—sell me new windows and siding."

Ethan grinned, until Nathan landed a sharp jab in Ethan's midsection. And then it was Nathan who grinned.

"Then Holly still hasn't called?" Marsh asked.

Mention of Holly as good as threw a switch. Nathan and Ethan straightened. Ethan rotated a shoulder; Nathan reached a hand to knead a muscle at the back of his neck. "I don't get it," he said.

"She's always on time for everything."

"She probably just got busy," Crystal said.

"When was she supposed to call?" Marsh asked.

"An hour and a half ago."

Crystal noticed that Ethan and Marsh exchanged worried looks. Marsh said, "Maybe you should call the hotel."

"I called an hour ago."

"And?"

"No one answered in the room. I spoke with someone at the desk. Nobody's seen Holly or Zack since eight o'clock this morning."

Marsh lowered his half-empty glass of water to the counter. Wanting to help, Crystal said, "Look, I've been to Boston. There's so much to do there. Holly's probably doing some of it. Maybe she's taking a tour or following the trail Paul Revere took or visiting a museum. Perhaps she made a friend, and is in her room, talking about boys and makeup. Just because Boston is a large city doesn't mean something bad has happened to her there."

"What sort of bad things?" Nathan asked.

Crystal's eyes widened. Leave it to a man to completely ignore her point.

"Muggings," Ethan said.

"Murder," Marsh declared.

"And mayhem," Ethan added.

"I doubt it's any of those things," Crystal said, trying valiantly not to raise her voice.

"You doubt?" Nathan's voice rose in volume. "You doubt?"

He picked up the phone again. Ethan turned on the television just in case there had been a natural disaster out east and nobody had bothered to tell them. Marsh paced, no small feat for a man in a walking cast.

Nathan spoke into the phone. The second he hung up, Marsh, Ethan and Crystal turned toward him. He shook his head. "I knew I shouldn't have let her go."

"Nathan, you're overreacting."

"Spoken like someone who's never had a child."

A place inside Crystal cracked open. She turned her back on the Quinn men so they wouldn't see the hurt on her face.

"I promised Mary I'd keep that girl safe."

"This waiting," Marsh said.

"This wondering," Ethan declared.

"This worrying," Nathan added.

"Try not to let your imagination run away with you," she said.

"You're a counselor, Crystal," Nathan said. "From what I hear, you're a darn good one. But you don't know anything about being a parent."

Sometime during his little speech, she'd turned around. She looked him in the eye, her hurt real, the enormity of it hovering just below the surface. "Don't be too quick to assume you know me."

She felt three pairs of eyes on her. She wanted to back up ten minutes. She hadn't intended to let that slip. Now, she didn't know what to say to undo it.

The phone rang.

Everyone jumped.

Nathan snatched it up. "Yeah, Holly, it's me."

Finally she looked at Ethan and Marsh. "I guess that's my cue to leave."

She gathered up her dishes. Head held high, she strode out to the sunporch and walked out the door.

Crystal sat on the edge of the bed, a tissue in one hand, the picture of her baby in the other. She'd cranked up the old Victrola before coming upstairs. It had run out some time ago. Still, she sat, unmoving. Remembering.

She pressed a hand to her flat stomach. There wasn't a single stretch mark. She knew because she'd searched years ago. She had one of those bodies made for giving birth. And yet she'd never had another child.

A shudder rose up inside her, but her eyes remained dry. She hadn't cried a tear through eighteen hours of labor, either. And then she'd cried when she'd least expected for nearly a year.

There was no describing the emptiness she'd felt. It was

strange, too, because she'd felt empty most of her early life. She'd been a rebellious child, too bright for her own good. Unfortunately, she'd spent too much time searching for love and acceptance, and not enough time reaching her potential. At least, that's what her mother was wont to say. To this day she didn't know what had propelled her into the arms of one of her professors, her mother's shrewlike tendencies or her father's complete and utter lack of emotion.

Professor Geoffrey Winslow had shown plenty of emotion. Twenty years her senior, he'd been newly divorced, animated, dashing and bright, and completely dedicated to his students. Or so she'd thought. She'd loved him with all the heart, mind and soul an eighteen-year-old girl could muster. She hadn't even been terribly worried when she'd realized she was late. She'd gone to Geoffrey the moment she was sure. His face had turned stone cold. Recovering, he'd taken out his checkbook.

Crystal matured ten years while he scribbled out the check that would fix everything. She'd torn it in half in front of his face, threatening to go to the dean. Calm and collected, Geoffrey had reminded her of her reputation, and asked her whom she thought the dean would believe.

He was right. The dean seemed to think she should have taken Geoffrey up on his most generous offer, and suggested she go to one of her boyfriends for help. Crystal felt as if she'd been slapped. She didn't have any boyfriends. With no place else to turn, she'd turned to her mother, newly widowed by then. Claire Galloway's slap hadn't been figurative. It had left a handprint on her cheek. A knife wouldn't have cut Crystal deeper.

Basically her mother washed her hands of her only daughter that day. But first she drove home all Crystal's inadequacies, all her mistakes, saying she'd embarrassed her mother for the last time. Crystal screamed at her, saying she would never be the kind of mother she'd always been.

Claire had laughed. "You're out of control and always have been. What in the world do you have to offer a child?"

That had hurt more than everything else combined. Years later Crystal had realized it had been her mother's own disappointments and inadequacies talking—transference they called it in psychology class. Penniless, Crystal had set off on her own, determined to be everything her baby needed. Ultimately, she feared her mother was right. If Crystal had been older. If she'd had a degree, a means of support for her and her child. If she'd had one person to count on.

If she hadn't seen families every place she went.

They were everywhere. Happy families, normal families, busy families, families that included fathers. She began grappling with her decision to keep her child. The thought of giving up the one person in all the world who might love her unconditionally made her ache in a way she'd never ached before. And she'd ached plenty.

If only things could have been different.

How many nights did she go to sleep, her mother's words playing through her mind. "You're out of control, Crystal. Out of control. Control."

She was hungry much of the time. And cold. And lonely. And the thing was, she didn't have control over any of those things. But she had control over one important issue.

Her child's future.

Oh, God, her baby.

She wanted her baby so badly. She wanted to do what was best for her child. And she just couldn't give her baby the best. She made the painful decision to give her baby to a family that could. She had a few stipulations. The potential mother and father had to be good, law-abiding citizens. They had to be part of the working class. They had to be dedicated to each other, and deeply in love. And they had to be young. She wouldn't allow some stodgy old couple to raise her child.

She only asked for one other thing. She wanted a photograph of her baby after a year. She wanted proof that her child was thriving.

She would never forget the day the photograph had arrived in the mail via the attorney who had handled the semiprivate adoption. The baby was beautiful, as Crystal had known she would be. Perhaps as poignant as the baby's smile, were the words delicately scrawled on the back. "Bless you."

Those two words had changed Crystal's life. She stopped drifting. She stopped fighting the system and her own intelligence. She went back to college. This time she applied herself. She won awards, scholarships. Finally she was blessed with a goal: to be the best she could be and to help others be the same.

Life had gone on, and she was still trying to accomplish those goals. Sighing, Crystal placed the framed photo on the table and went downstairs.

Part of her wasn't surprised when Nathan knocked on her door two hours later. Part of her had been expecting him. The more cowardly part of her wished she'd have been gone so she wouldn't have to deal with the dull and disquieting feelings of inadequacy and uncertainty plaguing her. It reminded her of everything she'd done wrong in her life.

She waited until the second knock to answer the door. Nathan stood outside, hat in hand, his expression somber. She stared at him in silence for what felt like a long time.

He stared back at her, his face implacable. Eventually one corner of his mouth twisted upward. It was more of a grimace than a smile—self-deprecating and cynical. "I've apologized more today than I usually do in a year. You were right about Holly. She and Zack were invited to a party after rehearsal. She's having the time of her life. She said some woman's after Zack. They had a cappuccino together.''

"I suppose you blame me for introducing him to cappuccino.''

A muscle worked in his jaw. "I probably deserved that.''

Crystal didn't know what he expected her to say. Nothing came to mind.

He smiled without humor. "I'll take those forty lashes now.''

"Just forget it, Nathan.''

His eyes narrowed. "I can't forget it, dammit.''

"Dammit, stop swearing at me.''

He took a deep breath. "I can't forget anything about you. I can't forget the way you looked when you were holding the Buchanan baby last week. And I can't forget the way you looked a few hours ago when you told me not to assume I knew you.''

It was her turn to sigh, her turn to shrug and swallow convulsively. "Nathan, look...''

He was looking. And what Nathan saw was a woman whose green eyes, normally brimming with excitement and tenderness, were flat and unreadable as stone. "You weren't speaking hypothetically, were you, Crystal?''

She stared at him for what seemed like forever and then she shook her head.

"Then you know how it feels to be a parent.''

Crystal wanted to walk away. She didn't want to get into this. She might have entrusted him with more of her secret before, but now she didn't have the heart for it. "Look,'' she said. "I was a mother. Once. For a few, short hours. A long time ago.''

Nathan's sigh was at one with the wind in the mulberry bushes outside. "I know better than anybody how trite words can be at a time like this. May I come in?''

Her brain told her to say, "No!'' Somehow, the command got short-circuited between her lips and her hand, which flattened against the door and gently pushed it open.

"I feel I owe you an explanation," he said, looking uncomfortable in the feminine room. He fiddled with his hat. "I don't know where to begin. I know it doesn't justify my actions, but something I don't much like squeezed into me when I saw you laughing with Marsh."

It was sheer will alone that forced her gaping mouth shut. "I don't understand."

"Marsh didn't leave Jasper Gulch because this house was pink. He left because he loved Mary."

"Zack said everyone loved Mary."

He shook his head. "Everyone loved Mary. But Marsh was in love with her."

"You mean they—"

"God, no. She had eyes only for me. We were all just kids, and besides, he would never have…well, anyway. I'm not so sure she made the best choice. Now you know why I reacted the way I did back at the house."

"Are you telling me you were jealous of Marsh because I took a short walk with him?"

"Let's just say it brought back old insecurities. I took it out on you."

She didn't say anything.

So he added, "I was thoughtless."

She nodded.

"Unfeeling."

She shrugged.

"A jerk."

This time she simply stared at him.

And he said, "You can jump in and disagree anytime." After another stretch of silence he said, "I told you I'm not perfect."

She turned away from him and strolled to the other side of the room. She'd changed out of her jeans and into a comfortable-looking dress in a mossy-green fabric that swished around her knees when she walked, lamplight catching in its folds.

She turned again, her hair long and loose and wavy down her back. From this distance it looked darker. She reminded him of someone. He couldn't say who.

"It's all right, Nathan."

"Are you saying you forgive me?"

"Yes. You're forgiven. I don't see any sense in both of us beating you up." Crystal smiled. She hadn't planned to. She didn't even want to. But she couldn't help herself.

"Marsh is a good man."

"He's charming, yes," she agreed.

"So you said." He shook his head, raked his fingers through his hair.

"Marsh isn't interested in me, Nathan."

He looked skeptical.

"Nor I in him."

His eyes filled with a curious longing. "You aren't?"

She shook her head.

The next thing she knew, he'd blazed a trail across the room, grasped her by the shoulders and hauled her into his arms. And he kissed her. It wasn't soul deep or tender, but swift and hungry. And then, as if he didn't trust himself, he thrust her away from him, turned on his heel. "Good night, Crystal." Without another word he walked out the door.

Crystal followed as far as the porch. It was a long time before she lowered her fingers from her lips, went inside and closed and locked the inner door.

Chapter Six

Crystal was still in a daze hours later. She'd taken a long, soothing bath, brushed her teeth, combed and braided her hair. She'd crawled between her lavender-scented sheets and closed her eyes. They only opened again.

Turning on the light, she went over the events and details of the entire day. She wasn't sure what had happened between her and Nathan. But something had.

Sighing, she reached up and turned out the light. Seconds later the telephone on the bedside table rang.

She placed the phone to her ear, and before she could speak, a deep, masculine voice said, "Elsa."

She would have assumed somebody had the wrong number, except she recognized that voice. "Nathan?"

"It can't be Nathan. Your shingle clearly depicts an *E*."

"How did you know I was still awake. Were you watching my window?"

"I still am."

She sat up in bed and moved the lacy curtain aside. The moon was a sliver in the black sky. She could see the mercury light on the barn in the distance, but Nathan's house was dark. "Which room is yours?" she asked.

Just then a light flicked on and off again in a room on the first floor. "Eunice."

She smiled, staring at the place the light had been.

"Edna."

"I'm not telling you."

"Ellen. Elizabeth."

"If my parents had named me Ellen or Elizabeth, I would be using that name."

"Estelle."

"Good night, Nathan."

"Crystal. Wait."

"Yes?"

"I had fun today. Earlier, I mean."

Her heart felt top-heavy and two sizes too big. If he didn't stop soon, it was going to tip over sideways in her chest and slide right into her stomach. "I did, too. Earlier, I mean."

"Before I turned into a jerk," he said.

"You were worried."

"I shouldn't have said the things I said."

Her heart teetered on her breastbone.

"And I was thinking that maybe you'd let me make it up to you."

"That isn't going to be easy."

His laughter nudged her heart. "You have no idea how much I was hoping you'd say that." He laughed again, and her heart tipped right over. "Do you have plans for tomorrow?"

"Nothing that can't be altered."

"You cooked for us tonight. Why don't you come over for dinner tomorrow, and I'll return the favor?"

"I thought you said it was called supper."

"Supper's at six Monday through Saturday. Dinner's at one on Sunday."

She was smiling when she said, "Dinner sounds lovely."

"I would reserve judgment until after you've tasted my cooking, if I were you. Eloise?"

She laughed. "Not even close."

"I'll see you tomorrow, E. Crystal. Good night."

She replaced the phone on the small bedside table. Pulling the covers under her chin, she stared at the ceiling. The breeze fluttered the curtains, weak moonlight dancing in delicate patterns on the far wall. Snuggling deeper into her pillow, she sighed.

And that's when she knew. She was falling in love.

Crystal ruffled through the papers spread out on her small kitchen table. She'd jotted a note or two when she'd first placed the file next to her steaming cup of coffee. Grover and Pamela Sue Andrews had an appointment for another counseling session Monday afternoon. Saving their marriage was an ongoing challenge, but since they seemed to truly love each other, Crystal was determined to do everything she could to help them. Her gaze strayed to the top of the piano where she'd arranged her metronome collection first thing this morning, then out the window, the notes she'd been trying to make sense of forgotten.

Smiling for no apparent reason, she groped for the mug and lifted it to her lips. Cold coffee slid down her throat. Shuddering, she made a face. She'd been daydreaming, and evidently had been for some time.

Daydreaming. She never did that.

A breeze wafted through the open window, ruffling the papers she'd been pretending to organize. It was no wonder she couldn't concentrate. It was spring. The mulberry bushes were in blossom, the clusters of white flowers pretty, their scent sweet. The air was warm and fragrant. And she was in love. The idea caught in the hollow between her breasts as it had last night after Nathan had called. It was a good thing she'd swallowed the coffee, because she would have choked on it if she'd tried it now.

In love?

It was one thing to be falling in love, or on the brink of love. Being *in* love was something else entirely.

She couldn't be in love with Nathan. Could she? The question quavered from its hiding place in the farthest corner of her mind.

She hardly knew him. She desired him. But that was different. People didn't have to know one another well to desire each other. Yes, she wanted him. That much she was sure of. What else could this gentle warming, this soft, languorous yearning mean?

She also *liked* him. Really and truly liked him. The therapist in her argued that if she knew him well enough to really and truly like him, it was possible that she knew him well enough to love him.

No wonder she couldn't concentrate. Love was dangerous.

Nathan was still grieving his late wife, for heaven's sake. So? she asked herself. She'd counseled people who had grieved an old love while discovering a new one.

Was that what he was doing?

A sense of urgency reared up inside her. Suddenly she knew what was really bothering her. It wasn't that she might be falling in love with him. It was that he might not fall in love with her in return.

That was what made him dangerous. She'd known it the first moment he'd burst through the hedge outside of the high school. It wasn't the threat of murder and mayhem. It wasn't anything he'd done. It was how he made her feel. With him she felt pretty. With him she felt witty. With him she felt young and free. And feeling like that scared her, because with him she felt as if she could be herself. For much of her life people hadn't liked her much for that.

They liked her IQ. They liked her test scores. Some liked her body. But other than a few friends she'd made along the way, no one had ever really delved through the layers of her personality to discover the person she was on the inside. It had taken years to admit how much her parents' coldness had hurt. Maybe she was stronger because of it, or in spite of it. She just didn't know. One thing she knew for sure was that if any man ever loved her, he was going to love her for herself and not something or someone he wanted her to be.

Crystal looked at her watch. It was only eleven o'clock. Nathan had specifically told her Sunday dinner was at one.

She swept her notes together, slid them into the file and stored them in the old-fashioned satchel hanging over the back of her chair. That done, she flattened her hands on the top of the table and slowly stood. What now?

She was who she was, complete with all her sharp edges and flaws and maybe even a few vulnerabilities thrown in for good measure. The funny thing was, she thought, gazing out the window again, Nathan had his sharp edges, too. He'd admitted as much when he'd let her know that he'd been jealous of Marsh when she'd been laughing with him.

She didn't know what had gone on between Mary and Nathan and Marsh all those years ago, but she didn't have to sit idly by while Nathan wondered if it was possible that history might repeat itself.

She smoothed her hands down her magenta-colored chinos, checked her hair in the mirror, excitement whirling through her all the while. She was going to make a stand. She didn't know exactly how she would do that, but one thing was sure: she couldn't do it from here.

Ten minutes later she stepped off the gravel road and into the Quinn yard. Unlike several other ranch houses in the area, the Quinns' wasn't far from the road. It was large, old and inviting.

She started toward the porch when a voice called, "Hey, Crystal. We're out here!"

Most of the buildings were hidden from view by the big house, but she could just see the edge of the corral where Ethan was perched on top of the fence, a lasso in one hand, his cowboy hat in the other. Skirting the porch, she ambled closer. Marsh stood a dozen feet from Ethan, his casted ankle resting on a low board. Clamping a piece of prairie grass between his teeth, he winked at her and said, "Soon as Ethan here learns how to rope a stationary target, I'm going to teach him to rope a moving one."

Ethan called his brother a string of unbrotherly sounding names. Marsh only grinned. "Care to learn?" he asked Crystal.

A movement out of the corner of her eye kept her from replying immediately. Nathan had stepped outside the doorway of the barn, jaw square, his hat tipped forward, his eyes in shadow.

She'd come here to make a stand. It was uncanny how an opportunity had presented itself. Moseying slightly closer to Marsh, she said, "I appreciate the offer." As if the wink she gave him wasn't blatant enough, she sashayed toward Nathan and added, "But I do believe I would rather learn to drive Nathan's motorcycle."

Behind her, Ethan sprang from the fence to the ground, laughing. A ruckus ensued. She could picture the elbow jabbing that was undoubtedly taking place, but her eyes were trained on Nathan. "That is," she said, giving him a smile she hoped went straight to his head, "if you'd care to teach me."

Nathan spread his feet a more comfortable distance apart and simply stared at Crystal. He would bet his favorite horse that somewhere in the dark recesses of her mind, she knew exactly what she was doing. Beyond her, Ethan and Marsh were busy making hand gestures that harked back to when they were kids. Back then Nathan would have enjoyed pounding them for it. Today he was too busy enjoying Crystal's flirtations.

The thought brought his chin down and his eyebrows up. She was flirting with him. Didn't that beat all? The tightening in his throat and the chugging in his chest weren't new. Those had been happening at regular intervals for more than two weeks now. Ever since the first time he'd held her in his arms when she'd been giving that self-defense demonstration at school.

"What do you say?" she asked.

"You're early."

"Does that bother you?"

They were back to that, were they? "Do I look bothered?"

She took advantage of the opportunity he'd given her and looked him up and down and back up again. "You look like the smoldering, rugged sort of man who could make his living selling everything from blue jeans to pickup trucks to cigarettes."

"I quit smoking years ago."

"So did I."

Her eyes held his. Smiling, she sashayed closer.

In a voice quiet enough so only she would hear, he said, "A man would get arrested for looking at a woman the way you're looking at me."

"That depends on the woman, and on the man. I know I'm early. Are you surprised to see me?"

Nathan considered his answer. The color of the woman's clothes was hard to miss. Magenta and orange. He'd spotted her a quarter mile away. Which was about how close she had to be before he reacted to her. From a distance, the attraction was like the low vibration of a guitar string being slowly strummed. Up close, it was more like the buzz he felt when he walked too close to an electric fence.

"Would you really like to learn to ride my motorcycle?"

"I'd love to, thank you."

There was absolutely no reason to suddenly feel seventeen again. Nathan half expected Marsh and Ethan to yell out something crude about the new spring in his step. There were snickers behind them, but no taunts were forthcoming as he and Crystal walked to another building and ducked inside.

He led her to a shadowy corner in the toolshed. While their eyes were still adjusting to the dim interior, he hauled the bike around and slowly pushed it outside. There, he pointed to the throttle, the brake, the clutch, running through the purpose of each. She asked an occasional question, nodding when he answered.

"Is there anything you don't understand?"

She swung a leg over the seat. When she wiggled her hips to get a feel for the machine beneath her, Nathan had to look away.

"Start her up!" she called.

"Are you sure?"

"Theory's okay, but there's nothing like actually doing something, is there?"

Nathan stepped down on the kick starter and told himself not to go where his fantasies had suddenly taken him. She put it in gear, slowly rolling away. She made it about three feet before stalling, trying to get out of low gear.

Marsh and Ethan were both watching from the corral as Nathan showed Crystal how to start the bike on her own. This time Crystal got the timing between the clutch and the throttle right, and she putted away from Nathan. She made two passes through the yard, one around the house and another past Marsh and Ethan, who swiped their hats off their heads and waved them at her. Nathan chuckled, enjoying himself immensely.

She pulled up beside him, her stop a little jerky. "What do you think?" he asked.

"Piece of cake. Hop on."

He considered telling her it was more difficult to balance

the motorcycle with two, but she was bright and undoubtedly already knew that. Besides, what was the worst that could happen at fifteen miles per hour?

He swung on behind her, and they putted away, his arms gliding around her waist, her back warm against his chest. "How far are we going?" he asked.

Her laughter rang out, sultry and vibrant on the warm spring air. "I guess that depends. How far do you want to go?"

"All the way," he said before he could stop himself.

Crystal's hand went slack on the throttle, and the bike nearly stalled. Inside, her heart jump-started.

"Easy," Nathan said in her ear.

They were on the road, and a car was coming. She slowed down even more, heading for the grass growing along the side of the road. The tires slipped in the loose gravel, and she swerved. Between the two of them, they managed to keep from tipping over, but not from laughing out loud. Not even the pinched expression on Harriet Andrews's face as she gave them a wide berth, practically taking the ditch on the other side of the road, could chase away the anticipation and the heady sense of urgency swirling through Crystal.

They weren't far from her house. The sun glinted off the upstairs windows and cast a glow on the pink house, making it look as if it was blushing. It beckoned, reminding her of a smiling old lady in a big hat.

Crystal navigated the driveway. Veering through the yard, she steered around the petunias and marigolds she'd planted, stopping in the shade beneath the apple tree behind the house. She cut the engine and said, "Who was Hester?"

"Hester?" He left his hands, big and warm, on her waist, as if he liked them there.

"You called this Hester's place. Is she the one who

planted the mulberry bushes and had the house painted pink?''

"Pink. The Ladies Aid Society claimed it looked like a house of ill repute. She was my great-aunt, my grandfather's sister, but we all just called her Hester. She liked it that way.''

"Was she married?''

He finally lowered his hands and got off the motorcycle. Holding it while she did the same, he answered, "No. Hester was way ahead of her time. Claimed she never needed a man, although there were rumors that she'd had an affair with someone she met out east.''

"You never knew for sure?''

He shook his head. "She never said. And that wasn't the sort of thing a person asked Hester. She was no shrinking violet, that's for sure.''

Nathan secured the motorcycle on its stand, then studied the house. Except for the crumbling rocks in the fence surrounding it, and the bushes that had overgrown their boundaries, the place hadn't changed since he was a kid.

"What did she look like?'' Crystal asked.

"I guess you could say she looked like her house. She was on the tall side for a woman. She was eccentric and wore big hats year-round. She drove a car back when it was fashionable to let men do the driving. And she loved to make the new members of the newly formed Ladies Aid Society sputter. They all turned their noses up at her. Of course, that was only because they couldn't force her to conform to their way of behaving and thinking.''

Crystal tested the stone fence closest to the apple tree. Finding it sturdy enough to hold her, she leaned against it. "I think I would have liked her.''

"I think she would have liked you, too.''

The simple compliment warmed Crystal in ways that surprised her. She'd lived without approval for a long time.

She'd told herself she didn't need or want it. She wanted it now. "What about you, Nathan?"

Nathan settled one boot on a rock at the base of the stone fence. "I was crazy for the old bat."

Crystal's smile was so tentative it made Nathan realize he'd misunderstood the question. It made him want to reach out and touch Crystal, to hold her hand and watch her smile grow.

"You're like her."

She looked surprised. But it was true. Hester had loved bright colors, too. Crystal's magenta slacks and magenta-and-orange-striped top would have looked garish on anybody else. The colors called attention to her, flashing like a neon sign, and yet the style and fit was lovely, the light in her eyes subdued, artful and serene.

"Maybe," he said, "I'm a little crazy for you, too."

A bird twittered high in the apple tree. Much closer, Crystal's breath caught in her throat. She felt a little bit hollow, a lot mesmerized. She felt wanted, desired and desirable. And warm. Lord, yes. It wasn't a warmth born of the sun, but one that started inside, radiating outward, melting her knees, her belly, her heart.

It was love. With all its dangers, in all its finery. It was love.

Tilting her head slightly, she whispered, "What would it take to make you sure?"

He swiped his hat off his head. "I don't want..." His voice trailed away.

Bravely she held his gaze. "What do you want, Nathan?"

He slid his fingers into her hair, slowly turning her head, drawing her chin up. "I want to kiss you."

The very air they breathed heated somehow. Her eyes were wide open. His were half-closed.

"And unless you tell me not to in the next five seconds, that's exactly what I'm going to do."

"Five," she whispered.

He lowered his face. "No fair playing hard to get."

She smiled. "Four."

"Three," they said in unison, their lips a hairsbreadth apart.

"Make that four seconds," he said as his mouth covered hers.

Everything inside her began to swirl together in a slow, smooth spiral. All her thoughts turned to oblivion. All her needs became one. Him. The breath rushed out of her a third time. She didn't gulp in another. Instead, she breathed him in, his scent, his breath, his heat and fire and passion.

She was holding on to him tight, with everything she had, and she still felt as if she were coming apart at the seams. He was having no such problem. His fingers were deft. It was as if her buttons had fallen out of their buttonholes, leaving her shirt gaping, the upper swells of her breasts exposed. And then his hands were covering her breasts, and his lips were pressed to her neck, moving lower, one kiss at a time.

She arched toward him, moaning softly.

"I remember hearing that a bullet meant for Nick Colter had grazed your skin."

For a moment she didn't fathom where he'd come up with that particular memory. Then she remembered the scar and realized he must have noticed it on her shoulder. "That was the day Kipp Dawson showed up in town to teach Nick a lesson." She sighed, and he kissed the scar. "Luckily, Nick's brother burst through the door and created a diversion."

"There were rumors about you and Nick's brother."

Her eyes were still closed, sunlight dancing beyond her eyelids, another sigh rising out of her throat as her hands spread wide on his chest. "They were only rumors," she whispered. "I didn't move here to find a man. I certainly didn't move here to follow one out of town."

"Why did you move here, Crystal?"

The breeze didn't stop blowing, the birds didn't stop singing, the world didn't stop spinning. But the question struck a chord, just the same.

Why had she come here? The answer was straightforward, but the issue was complicated. She'd alluded to the fact that she'd had a child. She'd only said that much because she'd been hurt. Apparently, he'd assumed her child had died, and she'd let it go at that. She didn't know how to tell him differently now.

He must have taken her silence as an indication that some things were private, because he straightened. As if it required an iron will, he dragged his gaze away from her breasts.

Leaning over to pick up his hat, he said, "We should be getting back."

She didn't want to go back. She wanted to take his hand, and lead him inside, up the narrow staircase to the red rosebud bedroom where she slept.

"I don't have protection," he said when she failed to second the idea of leaving. "I haven't needed it in years. I didn't plan this, but then, things like this usually aren't. Planned, that is. Unless you're protected?"

Crystal's fingers stilled on the third button. She knew she shouldn't smile, but she couldn't help it. He wanted her. And if she'd had the necessary provisions, they might have taken this to the next step. She shook her head, then ducked it, hiding her smile. "I haven't needed it in a long time, either, Nathan."

She grinned openly at the probing query that came into his eyes. "I was referring to protection, not sex. So you can relax."

A muscle worked in his jaw. "Relax? Ha!"

She laughed out loud. She couldn't help it. "What do you say we go back to your place, cowboy? You promised me lunch."

"I promised you dinner."

"So you did. Come on, I'll drive."

The wind picked up, fluttering the new leaves in the trees. Branches scraped against the house, the sound reminiscent of a mandolin, the notes carried away as if on a pleasing sigh.

Crystal noticed Marsh and Ethan as soon as she pulled into the driveway. They were standing two feet apart. Ethan's cowboy hat lay upside down on the grass at his feet. Marsh's was askew on his head.

"What are they doing?" she asked.

"Looks like they're bickering again."

They came to a stop, and Crystal turned the engine off.

"You boys having fun?" Nathan called.

Marsh answered without looking. "I'm about to chew our little brother up and spit him out in pieces."

"You and whose army?" Ethan retorted, poking a sturdy finger into his brother's chest.

"What's wrong?" Crystal asked, hopping off the motorcycle.

"Who said anything's wrong?" Ethan asked.

Marsh gave him a shove backward. Nervously skirting the pair, Crystal said, "Then this is just an explosion of testosterone?"

"Hell no! It's just a couple of guys letting off steam!" Marsh scoffed. "What do you think a testosterone explosion is, you idiot?"

That did it. Ethan lunged at Marsh, and the two toppled to the ground.

"Nathan, do something."

Nathan maneuvered the bike well out of the way of his brothers, then simply stood, watching. Crystal looked sideways at him. He reminded her of a little boy peering through a toy store window. "You're itching to get in on it, aren't you?"

"Child's play," he said. "Marsh is just getting antsy to get back to work. Being idle drives him crazy. He's taking it out on Ethan. Who probably has it coming."

"He's a wimp!" Ethan said, rolling around on the ground. "He thinks he's got it rough just because he's wearing a little cast."

Marsh slammed his little cast into Ethan's shin.

Crystal almost smiled.

"By the way, Nathan," Ethan called, doubling over at the fist he took in the midsection. "I took the liberty of starting the grill."

Marsh, releasing his own oomph, said, "I wonder what kind of liberties he just took."

Crystal didn't bother straightening her hair. But she glanced down, making sure her shirt was buttoned correctly.

"Nathan's too old to take liberties," Ethan ground out.

"That's right," Marsh said.

Crystal was a little surprised Nathan didn't get in on the fight. She wondered if he was holding back because of her. "All right, you two," he said, securing the motorcycle on its stand. "That's enough."

He leaned over, hauling Ethan to his feet by the shirt. Marsh climbed as far as his knees.

"Feeling better?" Nathan offered him a hand.

Marsh took it as if to accept the help, only to give it a hard yank, which caught Nathan off guard. Nathan recovered, and Marsh winked, grinned. "We're just getting warmed up."

Ethan tackled Nathan from behind, shouting like a banshee.

"You asked for it," Nathan said as the three brothers went down in a tangle of arms and legs.

Cowboy hats went flying, fists pounding. Crystal stayed where she was, interested in the fight in a gaping, tourist sort of way.

"You're really just teasing each other, right?" she asked at the dust they were raising.

Somebody, she thought it was Marsh, said, "Teasing's for sissies."

"Yeah." Ethan caught Nathan around the neck in a headlock. "We're not sissies. We're guys."

"Guys, hell," Nathan said. "We're men, and men don't, oomph, tease."

"We wrestle," Marsh agreed.

"We take it outside. Dammit, Marsh, watch that knee."

"We fool around."

Ethan said, "Sometimes we break things."

"Like lamps."

"And limbs."

"Your poor mother!"

The fight began to wind down. Crystal didn't know exactly why. As far as she could tell, nobody had won. And yet the rolling around and taunting became less frenzied, coming to a gradual halt. Ethan and Nathan climbed blithely to their feet. Marsh's movements were slightly hindered by his cast. As far as she could tell, his ankle was still his only injury. All three of them began brushing dirt and grass from their clothes.

"Poor my...eye," Marsh said from his knees. "Mom was a lone queen in a kingdom of five enamored males."

"Then she never wanted one of you to be a girl?" she asked.

"Hell," Ethan said. "She wanted every one of us to be a girl."

Near laughter Crystal said, "She must have been thrilled when Holly was born."

Silence.

She'd been prepared for several replies. No reply wasn't one of them.

The filly whinnied. Farther away a calf bawled. Marsh climbed the rest of the way to his feet. Nathan tucked in

his shirt, and Ethan looked around for his hat. Other than
the creak of leather and the scuff of boots on the hard
ground, no one made a sound. Searching for a plausible
explanation, she said, "Did your parents live to see Holly
born?"

Was it her imagination, or had Nathan, Marsh and Ethan
cast furtive glances at one another? What was going on?
What had she stumbled upon this time? It didn't take a
genius to figure out there was something they weren't telling her. She wondered if it had something to do with
Marsh. What else could it be?

Before her imagination got completely away from her,
Nathan answered. "Mom died when Holly was two. She
had pneumonia of all things. Dad went from a heart attack
two years earlier."

Cowboy hats were picked up, brushed off, dents pounded
out. As if by rote, the hats were returned to their heads.
From this angle these three brothers looked amazingly
alike, dark hair, dark eyes, smoldering expressions. What
were they hiding?

"Smoke," Nathan said.

"What?" she asked.

"I smell smoke."

"The steaks." Marsh swung around, already hobbling
toward the house.

"What steaks?" Nathan asked, following.

"The steaks I put on the grill," Ethan exclaimed.

"Are on fire! You idiot!" Marsh yelled.

"I thought you said you took the liberty of starting the
grill," Nathan admonished.

"Guess I took a few more liberties than that."

Nathan and Ethan rushed forward. On his way by Crystal, Nathan quietly said, "I guess today's the day for taking
liberties."

The look in his eyes warmed her. It didn't, however, help
her understand him. It seemed the more she got to know

him, the more she liked him and the more questions she had.

Since Marsh walked slower, she fell into step beside him. Up ahead, Nathan opened the lid on the gas grill, sending smoke billowing toward the sky. While he tried to save dinner, she tried to understand what had just happened.

"Would you tell me something, Marsh?"

"I guess it depends on the question."

She glanced at the second oldest Quinn. She really did not understand the group dynamics of this family. "Does Nathan usually participate in your brotherly scuffles?"

"I don't get home much. Why don't you ask him?"

That was another thing. Why didn't Marsh come home much?

"One thing's for sure," he said. "Nathan's shedding his sackcloth and ashes, and I think we have you to thank."

She didn't get it. That hadn't sounded like a man who begrudged his brother happiness.

They'd reached the old fieldstone patio where Ethan and Nathan were arguing over the position of the picnic table. Of course, Marsh got in on the discussion. Crystal settled in a comfy chair, completely baffled.

Ethan was sure the steaks could be salvaged. "Steak," he said more loudly than necessary. "And salad and rolls. All easy to pronounce."

With a roll of her eyes, Crystal asked if he had any French dressing. Nathan chuckled, and Marsh ribbed Ethan. The subject of Holly and Nathan and Marsh and Mary was dropped, but not forgotten.

Chapter Seven

"Hey, Brandy!" One of the local cowboys shouted from a table by the diner's window. "Can we get refills back here?"

"I'll be back with a fresh pot in two shakes." The voluptuous young waitress's smile slipped a little as she hurried to the counter and returned with a full pot. Pausing for a moment at the table where Crystal sat with three of her closest friends in Jasper Gulch, she said, "You ladies care for dessert?"

"I'd like a slice of warm apple pie," Brittany Colter said.

"I need chocolate," Jayne Stryker declared.

"I'll have a slice of chocolate cake, too," Meredith said with a smile. "You might want to bring the whole cake for Jayne."

"Very funny."

"How about you?" the waitress said.

Crystal became aware of Brittany's eyes on her first. Bypassing Jayne and Meredith, she looked up at Brandy and said, "I'll have what they're having."

Brandy appeared perplexed. "The pie or the cake?"

Crystal, who wasn't really even hungry, smiled wanly and said, "The pie, thank you."

Brandy headed for the back table, and conversation resumed all around her. It was twelve thirty-five on Thursday, and all ten tables and several of the booths were occupied. Forks rattled, dishes clanked, voices rose and fell. The diner had changed hands a few times in the past few years, but the cooking hadn't changed. Brioche and chicken cordon bleu had never been on the menu. In fact, the menu hadn't changed in years, either. Every day's special might as well have been carved in stone. There was mesquite steak on Monday, meat loaf on Tuesday, rib-eye steak and baby potatoes on Wednesday, baked ham with scalloped potatoes on alternating Thursdays and three-siren chili on Fridays. A person could get a cheeseburger, fried chicken and sandwiches any day of the week.

Most of the turkey sandwich Crystal had ordered was still on her plate. She hadn't been hungry lately. She'd been so full of airy hopes and dreams she hadn't had room for food. She'd read about this strange phenomenon, but until recently, she had never experienced it herself.

She'd seen Nathan every day since they'd eaten charred steaks on Sunday. Anybody who believed ranching was a quiet operation hadn't seen one up close. A semitrailer filled with seed had pulled in one morning. The driver, Nathan, Ethan and Marsh had worked diligently to unload it. As soon as it pulled out, empty, a buyer from Aberdeen had pulled in to take a look at the herd. And that was only one day. Another day, inoculations were given, soil tested, prices documented, machinery greased and serviced. At one point, Crystal had marveled at the activity level. Nathan's reply had been, "Other than summer, fall and winter, spring is the busiest time of the year."

One afternoon they stole away to the barn, where Nathan showed her how to ride a horse. Her muscles were still sore from riding the large, docile beast named Matilda. Wednesday night they'd watched a movie from her collection. She'd seen the action-adventure spoof a dozen times. That night was the only time she could recall getting so carried away in a man's kiss that she didn't see the ending.

They talked at great length about several serious topics such as world peace and evolution and creation. Crystal had more college education to back up her views. Her knowledge didn't keep Nathan from telling her, point-blank, that her interpretation was wrong. She discovered that he was very opinionated. But then, so was she. They argued as much as they agreed, but they laughed most of all. Although he'd mentioned Mary from time to time, he hadn't gone into detail about the life they'd shared. Somehow, Crystal hadn't gotten around to asking him the questions that hovered in the back of her mind. She hadn't mentioned the child she'd once had, either. Perhaps she would one day, but for now, what they shared felt brand-new. And it really had nothing to do with either of their pasts.

A flash of silver caught her eye through the diner's window. Vehicle makes and models weren't her specialty, but she recognized Nathan's truck as he drove by. She continued staring out the window long after he disappeared. Someone had affixed a flyer advertising an upcoming dance to the old lamppost out front. Although it was spring now and not winter, the window and the view beyond it looked much as it had appeared in the photograph she kept on her nightstand.

Somewhere in the far reaches of her mind she was aware that the bell over the door had jingled several times, and the low drone of voices throughout the diner had changed. It was quieter now. Therefore, she should have had an easier time paying attention to the conversation taking place at her own table.

"...and I came across the most unusual metronome at

that estate sale today. I believe the writing on the bottom is in German. I know you're collecting them.''

Crystal wondered what time Nathan planned to stop over tonight. She was going to fix fondue, which was back in style.

''Crystal?''

The sound of her name drew her attention. Animated about something, Meredith grinned warmly and gestured with both hands. ''So I picked it up for you. You can take a look at it the next time you stop in at the store....''

''That's nice, Meredith.'' She peered out the window again, wondering where Nathan had gone. He'd stopped by last night, after keeping vigil over a calf that had gotten sick. He'd arrived on her doorstep, freshly showered, a simmering expression deep in his eyes.

''Crystal?''

She met her friend's gaze. ''Hmm?''

Meredith pushed her pale-blond hair behind her ears. ''Did you hear a word I said?''

Vaguely she recalled the words *estate sale*. Drawing on that, she said, ''You're going to another estate sale. Don't forget to watch for an antique metronome to add to my collection.''

Three pairs of eyes were suddenly on her.

''I knew it,'' Meredith said.

''She was daydreaming,'' Jayne added.

''I don't believe I've ever known her to daydream,'' Brittany Colter, who probably knew Crystal better than anyone, said.

''There's no need to talk about me as if I'm not even here,'' Crystal said drolly.

''You were miles away just now,'' Jayne reminded her.

Crystal shrugged.

''You were thinking about a man, weren't you?'' Meredith asked.

''Were you?'' Brittany asked, obviously surprised.

"That explains it," Jayne said, twirling a lock of her short, unruly dark hair. "The question is, who?"

Crystal glanced at her uneaten lunch, at the nearly full glass of iced tea. She considered asking her friends if they knew anything about the Quinns. But she absolutely abhorred gossip and decided against it. When the time was right, she would ask him herself.

Brandy brought their desserts. After that, Crystal's mind wandered again.

Jayne, Meredith and Brittany finished their lunches. "Are you coming?" Brittany asked.

Her three friends were waiting for her behind their chairs. Crystal stood, too, but more slowly. "You three go ahead," she said, digging in her purse for a tip.

The cowboys who'd been sitting under the window ambled out the door behind Brittany, Jayne and Meredith. Brandy disappeared into the kitchen. Suddenly Crystal realized that the only diners remaining were eight of the staunchest members of the Ladies Aid Society.

Oh, boy.

She strode to the counter near the front of the room, waiting for Brandy to return from the kitchen so Crystal could pay for her meal. A long time ago she would have ducked into the rest room or simply left the money on the counter. That was before Crystal realized a person couldn't run from adversity. She remained where she was, holding her ground and facing the music. Actually, her back was facing the music. And several pairs of eyes were boring holes into her this very second.

Great. The Ladies Aid Society was all she needed.

"I hear tell that dear Nathan Quinn has himself a little diversion."

"A what?"

"A mistress, dear."

"Not our Nathan!"

Crystal fought the urge to turn around, stride over to their table and tell them to mind their own business. She even considered telling them it wasn't true. They didn't know anything. But what good would it do? They believed what they wanted to believe.

"A mistress? Are you sure?"

"All I'm doing is reading the writing on the wall."

"Oh, my. Mary's only been gone a year. Do you think it's serious?"

Crystal recognized Edith Fergusson's distinctive voice. Unfortunately, she also recognized the whisper shrill enough to penetrate steel that followed. "Heavens no. I believe it's called a transitional woman these days."

"Oh, dear. Who is it, Harriet?"

"A lady, and I use the word loosely, of dubious background."

Suddenly, the silence was thick enough to cut with a knife. Crystal could well imagine the fingers pointing at her.

"I can hardly believe it."

"Believe it."

"I always assumed Nathan would look for a woman more like Mary."

"I'm sure he will when he gets this out of his system. After all, *he's* a wonderful, kind, sensitive man."

"Yes, he is all that and more."

"Like I told my Grover, this is just a passing fancy. You give him a few weeks, and he'll undoubtedly grow tired of, well, you know, and then he'll come to his senses."

Brandy returned from the kitchen, and the subject was dropped. The young waitress smiled kindly at Crystal. "Was everything okay?" she asked, punching the button on the old cash register. And then in a quiet voice she added, "I heard part of what was said from the doorway. Don't listen to them. They think they know everything about everybody. I doubt any of them would know what to do if a man with Nathan Quinn's legendary cowboy swagger ambled across their doorsteps. That man is like a box of chocolates, every layer luscious, smooth and delicious. If you're seeing him, I'd say you're lucky."

Crystal appreciated Brandy's vote of confidence. Still, it wasn't easy to dismiss the hurtful things Harriet and the others had said about her. That was what she got for daydreaming, she thought.

Chin held high, she walked out the door.

"You're up late."

Crystal didn't jump at the sound of Nathan's deep voice. She'd recognized his shadow the moment it fell across the grass growing near the porch steps. "I couldn't sleep."

"Neither could I."

Lowering the flute she'd been playing, she glanced all around. The moon was full, and so bright it cast shadows through the overgrown mulberry bushes. Nathan's truck wasn't parked in the driveway. That didn't surprise her, either. She would have noticed headlights. Peering into the yard, she searched for his horse.

"How did you get here?" she asked.

"I followed your music."

"You mean you walked over?"

"I have two legs."

That reminded her of Brandy's mention of Nathan's legendary swagger. Which reminded her of the gossip she'd spent the better part of the day trying to forget.

"Is something wrong?" His voice, at one with the late hour, drew her gaze. He stood at the foot of the porch steps, the toe of one boot balancing on the edge of the first step, the other foot firmly on the ground. His right hand was outstretched, a box of chocolates held loosely in his grasp.

"Did you know that Brandy Schafer described you as a box of chocolates this very afternoon?"

"Brandy's always been dramatic."

"People are starting to talk, Nathan."

"About what?" He went up one step.

"About you, and how your truck has been seen parked beneath my apple tree. *At all hours.*"

He went up another step. "What people?"

"Some of the women of the Ladies Aid Society."

He released a breath through pursed lips. "Hester always said the society was just a front that gave the members a license to gossip."

She felt herself responding to his no-nonsense attitude. "Then Mary wasn't a member?"

"Not an active one. She didn't like to make waves, but she steered clear of them as much as possible."

"They're linking your name with mine, Nathan."

He shrugged.

Before she completely gave in to the emotions swirling through her, she made one last valiant effort to warn him. "They describe you as a paragon of virtue and me as a two-bit hussy."

"I don't care what they say. Besides, they're wrong. There's nothing cheap or nonvirtuous about you. I wouldn't mind hearing how you describe me."

She placed her flute on the table next to the porch swing, the action causing the swing to sway side to side. She'd heard of fishing for compliments, but that really took the cake. And he didn't even have the grace to flush.

She'd had no intention of giving a running description out loud, but there was something about the warmth in his eyes and the barely there smile on his lips that made her say, "Dark hair. Dark eyes."

He slid the box of candy next to her flute. "Go on."

"Broad shoulders." Setting the swing in gentle motion again, she looked up. "Nice haircut."

"I took a lot of flack from Ethan about that. Anything else?"

Her smile was slow in coming. "Lean, chiseled, rugged and hard."

He reached for her hand, squeezed it and gave it a tug hard enough to bring her off the swing and to her feet. The next thing she knew, his arms were around her, and she had a very good idea how correct her description had been.

His mouth found hers, his hands molding her to the firm lines of his body. Every time he kissed her felt like the first time. Her breathing became shallow, her pulse sped up, and her thoughts turned as hazy as a long-forgotten dream. She'd kissed other boys over the years, and later other men. But not one of them had ever made her senses reel and her heart sing. Not even Geoffrey had made her feel this way. She stopped the thought right there.

Ah, Nathan thought. This was exactly what he'd needed. Dropping in on Crystal was becoming a habit, kissing her addictive. He dug in his heels and dug up some willpower. Setting her away from him, he adjusted his hat, which had a way of getting knocked askew whenever he was around her.

"Nathan?"

He hummed something that passed for yes.

"What was Mary like?"

That was the last thing he'd expected her to ask. But he supposed it was only natural that she was curious. "Mary was…" His voice trailed away, only to start up in the same place. "She was…everything. Funny, kind, smart, sweet to a fault, if there is such a thing, pretty. She used to chew on her lower lip and twirl her hair. She could cook and sew and bake, and she always complained if we forgot to put the toilet seat down."

"She sounds lovely."

"She was."

"Does Holly look like her?"

"No."

When he failed to expound on that, she said, "I've heard of yup and nope talkers. You must have written the guide-book."

He found himself reacting to Crystal's humor. He missed Mary. He didn't know what he missed the most. Her laughter? Or was it seeing her head bent close to Holly's? Talking about her usually hollowed him out. Lately the ache felt less raw.

The first moths of the season fluttered near the porch light. Other than the wind in the trees, the soft thud and swish of their wings was the only sound he heard. Crystal was studying him.

"What are you doing?" he asked.

"I'm trying to figure out what you see in me."

She held his eyes bravely, but Nathan wasn't fooled. Her fingers quivered, her entire body vibrating like a mouse cornered by a barn cat. She was taller than Mary by several inches. Maybe Crystal knew self-defense and was fluent in French, but in the ways of a woman she was no less vulnerable.

"You're beautiful, vibrant and exciting."

"Yeah, yeah, yeah."

"You are."

She waved his praises aside. Nathan was stumped. She had to know she was beautiful. A person couldn't look like her and not know that. A light came on. She wasn't insecure about her outward appearance.

He took a step closer, reached a finger to her chin and gently raised it. "The Odelia Johnsons and Harriet Andrewses of this town call you a two-bit hussy because they've never taken the time to look deeper. If they had, they would see that you're even more beautiful on the inside."

Her lips parted, and he was fairly certain she sighed. "Then you're not ashamed of me?"

"Are you crazy?"

"Maybe I am," she said.

"I'm not ashamed of you. Of course I'm not ashamed of you. Why would you think I'm ashamed of you?"

"Harriet Andrews said I'm a passing fancy."

"Harriet can take a flying leap."

She almost smiled. "Then you aren't trying to hide a candle beneath a bushel basket?"

"Of course not." Whatever the hell she meant.

"You're saying you wouldn't be embarrassed to be seen with me?"

He was beginning to understand. "I'd be honored."

"Feel like proving it?"

He shifted his weight to one foot, warming to the challenge in her eyes. "What did you have in mind?"

"I was thinking that perhaps you would want to put your money where your mouth is."

Nathan eased a little closer. She talked tough. Inside she was soft as dandelion fluff. His gaze trailed below her shoulders, then back to her face. Her eyes didn't so much as flicker. As if she knew he was thinking about where he'd like to put his mouth, she squared her shoulders and straightened her spine.

"If you're not ready, fine," she said. "If you are, prove it."

"Prove it."

Crystal could tell Nathan was grappling with her meaning. So she helped him out. "I mean go public."

"You want me to kiss you in public?"

She rolled her eyes. "Of course not. Well, I suppose that's up to you. But I was referring to the two of us being seen together in public. I was thinking more along the lines of a date."

"You want to go on a date? You and me?"

"Well, you and I."

One corner of his mouth lifted, hinting that he was about to smile. She warmed at least ten degrees, and his last compliment had already started her melting.

"What did you have in mind?" he asked.

"I don't know. Nothing too shocking or scandalous."

He eased even closer. "The Anderson brothers are coming home for a visit. I've seen flyers all over town advertising a dance Saturday night in their honor. Care to go?"

"With you?"

"The only other man awake at this hour is the man in the moon."

"I hear he's fickle."

"I guess that leaves me. I'll pick you up at eight."

She thought he might kiss her again. She'd thought wrong. She smiled, anyway. "I'm looking forward to it."

He inclined his head and, with a tug on his hat, turned on his heel. She watched until he disappeared from view on the other side of the mulberry bushes, listened until the thud and crunch of his footsteps could no longer be heard in the overgrown grass.

Gathering up her flute and the box of chocolates, she walked inside, closing the door behind her. A giggle bubbled up inside her, spilling over. The yup and nope talker had spoken from the heart. He thought she was beautiful, on the inside, where it mattered most. Their relationship just reached a new level. She performed a neat little pirouette, then danced a jig all the way up the stairs. She paused in her bedroom's doorway. Smiling, she breezed to the nightstand, lifted the framed photograph in both hands and waltzed around the room.

"You didn't tell me you could dance."

"I can stomp my feet as good as the next man," Nathan said. "Just don't expect me to attempt a waltz."

"Would you like to learn to waltz sometime?"

"Would I have to listen to classical music to do it?"

Crystal drew away from him slightly in order to see his face. Pleasure swirled in her stomach, gaining momentum. She was becoming accustomed to his tendency to answer her questions with questions. It was an unusual way to have a conversation. It made talking to him complicated, thought provoking and generally just plain fun. "I take it you don't like classical music?"

"Just a bunch of violins sawing away if you ask me."

"That sawing violin is one of the most difficult musical instruments to master. Since I showed no interest in it, my parents turned to dance. I was supposed to be a prima ballerina. Unfortunately, I wasn't thin enough as a child."

He uttered a word she would have been hard-pressed to spell.

"Is that why you listen to classical music?" he asked. "Because it was forced on you while you were growing up?"

"I listen to it because it's beautiful. It doesn't have this catchy beat, though."

He chuckled, and then she was being spun around. Crystal felt as if she was floating, and it had nothing to do with the music. Although she'd arrived with Nathan, she had been twirled around the room by several different partners. Nathan always appeared at the end of the song to claim the next one.

"Do you miss it?"

"Classical music?" she asked.

He steered them around a group of women line dancing. "Plays. Music. The opera."

She made a face that had gotten her in trouble when she was a child. "I would be highly suspicious of anyone who claims to miss the opera. Oh, don't underestimate its power. I admire the performers who master it, and I appreciate the degree of difficulty and drama. I'm amazed at the broad spectrum of notes its most talented singers reach, not to mention the volume behind the voices. But miss it? I would take a good book on a cozy swing anyday."

"Then this is all you want? This small-town life?"

His voice was deep, the big hand at her waist warm. She closed her eyes. She wanted this. And she wanted more. For now dancing with Nathan was enough.

She hummed an answer, and he tried to pull her closer. "Oh, no you don't. I'm not about to give the ladies of the society any more fuel for their gossip. You've already caused quite a stir, Mr. Quinn."

"You're causing the stir. You and that dress and those shoes."

She tipped her head back and laughed out loud, the sound lost in the noise of hands clapping and boots stomping all around them. Those closest were aware of the amorous attention Nathan Quinn was paying the Galloway woman. Half the men were envious. A few of the women commented that there was something familiar about Crystal tonight. They couldn't put their fingers on what it was.

There was nothing familiar about her dress. Crystal had found it in the back of her closet when she'd moved. It was simple in design, the color of bronze, not loose, not tight. Its neckline was deeply rounded, its hem brushed her ankles. Had it not been for the slits to her knees, she wouldn't have been able to move. Her shoes were brown, too, with square toes and heels that brought her within inches of Nathan's height. Or maybe she really was floating off the ground.

She'd fastened her hair on top of her head. Several strands had escaped the pins and were cascading down her neck and forehead. She wouldn't say she felt like a princess, but she felt very much a lady.

The town council had decided that the town hall was too small to contain the crowd that would undoubtedly gather to hear the Anderson brothers' music, especially now that the local boys had turned professional and were now living in Nashville. Crystal didn't know if Neil, Ned and Norbert, now called The Dakotas, would ever make it big, but the fine folks of Jasper Gulch sure thought so. They'd turned out in droves to hear the brothers tune their guitars and call do-si-do. Cletus McCully's barn was filled nearly to bursting. Which was about how Crystal's heart felt these days.

She and Nathan had arrived two hours ago. Nathan hadn't done anything about all the local cowboys who had cut in that first hour. After that, he cast a quelling glare at anybody daring enough to try. Clive Hendricks was the first who ignored it. He ventured close and tapped Nathan on the shoulder.

Crystal felt Nathan's arms tighten around her. Before they came to a complete stop in the middle of the dance floor, Ethan appeared out of nowhere. With a wink, he practically plucked Crystal right out of Nathan's arms and called, "You can thank me later!"

"You'd better behave yourself, Ethan."

"Shucks, Nate. Behaving's no fun."

Nathan watched until Ethan spun Crystal out of sight. Clive shook his head, then moved on to cut in on someone else. Since Nathan had no desire to dance with anyone else, he ambled to the sidelines. Eyeing the punch table, he decided to help himself to a cool drink.

He was polishing off his second paper cup full when Odelia Johnson jostled his arm. "Oh, excuse me, dear."

"No harm done, Odelia." If he hadn't happened to be looking, he wouldn't have noticed the look Odelia cast at Harriet Andrews, who was watching from a dozen feet away. If he hadn't happened to be looking, he might have been inclined to believe this little conversation hadn't been planned.

"When is that sweet girl of yours coming home?" Odelia asked, patting her springy white hair.

Nathan looked across the dance floor where Ethan and Crystal were doing a neat two-step. "She and Zack are flying in tomorrow."

"You must miss her terribly."

He hadn't wanted to let Holly go, and yet the week had gone by extremely fast. Holly had called every night. Crystal had been right. The girl was having the time of her life. When she wasn't sitting in on rehearsals, she was dragging

Zack to every deli and antique music store in Boston. Zack had said he never wanted to look at another dill pickle or have to listen to the tunes she played on old mandolins. The poor guy sounded exhausted and was ready to come home.

"Will things be returning to normal tomorrow?" Odelia asked.

"What do you mean by normal?"

It occurred to Nathan that that was something Crystal might have said. Suddenly, Odelia must have thought the same thing. She looked as if she'd just gotten a whiff of something smelly. "As her father, it's your duty to set a good example."

Nathan's temper flared.

"What do you think she'll say when she finds out her father's been carrying on with the likes of that...that woman?"

That-that woman chose that-that moment to glance Nathan's way, her smile lighting up the room. Nathan scooped his hat off his head, ran a hand through his hair and crammed the hat back in place. "If you have something to say, Odelia, say it. Otherwise..."

The old biddy smoothed her chubby fingers over her flowered dress. She reminded Nathan of a lion stalking prey two or three times its size. "Some people in this town have been spreading rumors. I don't believe them for an instant, mind you."

Nathan just bet.

"But some folks are saying that your truck's been seen parked in that Galloway woman's yard all hours of the night. I thought it only right to tell you what I've heard."

"First of all," Nathan said, his voice carefully controlled, "I'm not carrying on."

Odelia beamed. "That's what I thought. Why—"

"And second of all, Crystal isn't something you stepped in. She's a fine woman."

"Well, I'm sure you—"

"And as for how Holly will react?"

"Yes?" Odelia said dubiously.

"She's a delight. She's smart, talented and good. And kind. She has more common sense than most adults I know."

"Yes. Mary did a fine job with her. You, too, of course."

"Since Holly isn't a judgmental, finger-pointing bigot, I can't see how she could help but see the good in Crystal, can you?"

Nathan knew the exact moment his meaning sunk in. Odelia's double chin came up, and her eyes flashed with indignation. "Why, I never!"

Marsh strode over as Odelia bustled away to Harriet Andrews's side. One eyebrow raised, he said, "What's with her?"

"You don't want to know."

"Have you seen Ethan?"

Nathan glanced at Marsh. "He's dancing with Crystal. Why?"

Marsh started to walk away.

"Where are you going?"

The song ended about the same time Marsh shrugged one shoulder. "Someplace more exciting. Maybe I'll go watch some paint dry."

Ethan returned Crystal to Nathan's side. Snagging Ethan's arm, Marsh said, "I need a ride."

"A what?"

"Or your keys."

"My what?" Ethan asked.

"Are you deaf? I'm heading into town to the Crazy Horse. You want to go?"

Ethan started to tell Marsh the keys were in the ignition. At the last minute he glanced at Crystal and Nathan and then at the crowd that contained a noticeable lack of single women. Muttering under his breath, he went after Marsh.

Crystal watched them go. Their fuses were especially short tonight. She'd noticed that other people's tempers were high, too. She'd heard somebody blame it on the change in barometric pressure. A storm was brewing to the west. Electricity was definitely in the air.

Blowing a shock of hair off her forehead, she turned to Nathan. ''Having fun?''

''More fun than Ethan and Marsh.''

''Did you and Odelia have a nice chat?''

He scowled. ''Odelia Johnson could take the fun out of whistling. I put in a good word for you with the Ladies Aid Society.''

She studied his expression. His lips were parted slightly, his eyes crinkled at the corners, and not entirely innocent looking. The two gray-haired women guarding the punch bowl against potential spiking were shaking their heads in Nathan's direction.

''You probably shouldn't have done that,'' she said.

''I probably should have done more.''

The intensity in his eyes reached inside her, spreading to a place beyond her heart, a place she couldn't name. He'd come to her rescue, defending her name and honor. It reminded her of the first time she'd seen him up close. Men simply didn't do that for her. Nathan had, twice.

''What did you tell Odelia?''

''I didn't tell her anything, at least not outright. I might have hinted that she's a narrow-minded gossip and a bigot. Care for a glass of punch?''

Tears came out of nowhere, filling Crystal's eyes. Blinking them away, she took a small step closer, her gaze on his face. The music faded into the background, the crowd disappeared. ''Out of Odelia's punch bowl? No, thanks.''

''Do you want to dance?''

She shook her head. ''Do you?''

It was his turn to shake his head.

''What do you want to do?'' she asked.

His eyes darkened, a muscle worked in his throat. He wanted her. She'd known it all evening. She'd felt it in the way he held her, at the reluctance in his fingertips when someone had cut in.

"Does it seem crowded and noisy in here to you?" she asked.

He nodded.

"Would you like to find a quieter, less crowded place?"

She knew how provocative that sounded. She couldn't help it. She wanted what he wanted. Before they had what they both wanted, she needed to tell him her secret. Maybe their pasts didn't have anything to do with the present, but the past mattered.

Reaching up, she whispered in his ear. "There's something I'd like to talk to you about."

"You want to go someplace quiet to *talk?*"

She made a valiant effort not to smile and lost. She couldn't help it. She was happy...happier, perhaps, than she'd ever been before. "There's something I'd like to tell you. And then, if you still want to, maybe we could think of something to do that doesn't require talking."

Nathan crushed his paper cup. Clasping her hand in his, he cut a path through the crowd, making a beeline for the door.

Chapter Eight

"For someone who wanted to talk," Nathan said, "you're awfully quiet."

Crystal turned her face into the cool air streaming through the truck's windows. Stars had been out in the western sky when they'd first left the dance. Clouds had moved in fast, making it a pretty sure bet that the moon wasn't going to put in an appearance at all. Elvis serenaded them in the background. Her mother had forbidden Crystal to listen to Elvis when she'd been growing up, blaming him for the decline of morals in the entire western world. Suffice it to say, Claire Galloway never claimed to see Elvis at the mall.

"What are you thinking about?" Nathan asked.

"Elvis."

"You're kidding."

She smiled in spite of herself. "Well. Elvis and my mother."

Crystal's second smile was wry. She could well imagine her mother's reaction if she'd heard her name linked to that of the late Southern legend.

"Is that what you want to talk about?" he asked. "Your mother?"

Turning her head, Crystal studied Nathan's profile. Other than the lights on the dash, it was dark in the truck. Only his most prominent features were visible, the straight line of his nose, the sharp angle of his chin. "I suppose it always comes down to our mothers, doesn't it? My mother would scoff at the likes of Odelia Johnson and Harriet Andrews. And yet she would agree that I'm unworthy of someone like you, too."

"Someone like me?"

"A man who is an enigma and is close to perfect."

"I'm hardly perfect, Crystal."

But he was an enigma, and had been since the first time they'd met. It was highly likely that was one of the things that had drawn her to him initially. She'd fallen in love with much more than the enigma. Which was why she felt compelled to tell him about her past before their relationship reached the next level.

Okay, she thought. Where did she begin? While she was still pondering this, he said, "Did you want to go to your house to talk, or mine?"

They were only a mile from either place. Shrugging, she patted her purse where she'd tucked the purchase she'd made that very afternoon at a corner drugstore in Murdo. "Either house is fine."

Nathan couldn't remember the last time a woman had had so much trouble telling him what was on her mind. Yes, he could. The last time the air had been so taut with tension was the day Mary had told him she'd found a lump. He recalled another time, years earlier, when she'd told him she was pregnant.

He swallowed, and turned into Crystal's driveway. "Do me a favor and tell Marsh, Ethan and Zack how perfect I am. They seem to think I'm an ornery bear most of the time."

She feigned disgust. "Next you're going to tell me you don't always recycle."

He parked the truck in the driveway, turned the key, then sat motionless in the dark. "It's worse than that."

"Would it make you feel any better to know that my hair isn't really this shade of blond?"

He felt a smile lurking. "When nobody's looking, Ethan and I watch Jerry Spangler."

"I could be on Jerry Spangler's show."

"Don't tell me you used to be a man."

He'd expected her to punch him in the arm, or tell him what he could do with his assumption. Instead, she peered out into the darkness, and in a voice gone noticeably deeper, she said, "Actually, I could be on for a couple of different themes. I can hear the announcer now. 'Stay tuned to meet the girl who got herself kicked out of seven boarding schools in seven years.'"

"You're the one who said seven's lucky. What else did you do that could earn you a spot on Jerry's show?"

"I fell in love with one of my professors at university."

Just then, lightning ripped the center out of the sky. In the instant it flashed, Nathan glimpsed a deep sadness on her face. In the darkness that followed, he said, "Was he your baby's father?"

He had to watch closely to see her nod. He had to listen closely to hear her whisper. "He didn't want her."

"Your child was a girl?"

Again she nodded. Reaching for her hand, he opened his door. "It's starting to rain," he said. "You can tell me about her inside."

"Nathan?"

He stopped, half in, half out of the truck.

"You're closer to perfect than you give yourself credit for."

"You're not the only one who's made mistakes, Crystal. You aren't the only person who's faced a surprise pregnancy. Mary was pregnant when I married her. What do you say about that?''

She sighed. ''It seems this is the night for baring souls.''

His blood heated, the surface of his skin as electrically charged as the lightning dancing on the horizon. She must have known he was thinking about baring more than their souls, because this time she did give his hand a swat.

''I've heard of cowboys who take their love on the run, but you're not one of them. You did right by Mary. What is it they say? Second babies take about nine months to arrive, but first babies can come anytime. So what if Holly was born less than nine months after the wedding? At least her parents were married. It's more than Geoffrey offered me.''

Nathan was beginning to understand why Crystal had looked so sad when she'd held little Storm Buchanan that day a few weeks ago. She'd worn a similar expression a few days ago when she'd told him she'd had a child, once, a long time ago. He could only imagine what she'd been through with some man named Geoffrey. He had a sudden urge to wrap his arms around her and comfort her, to hold the great sadnesses of life at bay and keep her safe and warm and dry.

He drew her the rest of the way from the truck. The wind had picked up, flinging the first drops of rain into their faces as they made a mad dash for the porch. Her hand was poised over the doorknob when he said, ''Mary and I were married for eighteen years.''

Crystal didn't see the relevance of that bit of trivia. Nathan had spoken haltingly, almost reluctantly, as if guarding a secret. Something didn't add up. Before she could pluck one of the dozen questions that were scrambling through her mind, another pickup truck sped into her driveway.

Ethan rolled down his window. ''Marsh is packing.''

''What?'' Nathan asked. And then, ''Why?''

''He's leaving.''

"When?"

"He says tonight."

Nathan swore under his breath. "I thought he wanted to see Holly before he left."

Ethan swore, too. "You know Marsh."

Nathan looked from Crystal to Ethan. "Stall him until I get back."

Ethan rolled up his window and sped out of the driveway. Crystal finished unlocking her door. Once inside, she turned on an old lamp. She'd wanted to tell Nathan about her past. Now she felt on the verge of figuring out the answer to a confusing puzzle.

"Does what you're talking about have something to do with Marsh?"

"Marsh?"

The light she'd switched on cast a golden glow through the antique shade, throwing shadows in the corners. The shadows in Nathan's eyes were coming from within.

"You said he was in love with Mary."

Nathan shook his head very slowly.

She forged ahead on tiptoe. "Marsh said he doesn't come home often. Even Ethan thinks that's strange."

"That has nothing to do with Holly."

"How do you know?"

"I know, Crystal."

"I mean," she said, steadily drawing closer, "I'm not judging Mary. God knows I've made my share of mistakes."

"Mary didn't make a mistake, dammit."

Crystal opened her mouth to remind him that he was the one who said no one is perfect. Nathan cut her off before she could get a sound out. "She didn't sleep with my brother. I'm one hundred percent sure."

She knew she should stop there. When had that ever kept her from continuing? "No one can be one hundred percent sure. Except Mary. And Marsh."

"I'm sure."

"But how…"

"You think Marsh is Holly's biological father? Is that what this is all about?"

"I didn't say that. I said perhaps."

"He isn't."

"But…"

"There's no perhaps about this. He isn't. I know because Mary didn't give birth to Holly."

Lightning struck. Close this time. Thunder shook the entire house. The lamp flickered off, then on again.

The storm was closing in on them. Crystal was closing in on the truth. "But you said Mary was pregnant when you married her."

"She was. She lost that baby. We were young, broke, scared. I didn't get her medical attention soon enough. She didn't want to go to the doctor. I should have insisted. I should have dragged her there if I had to. There were complications. By the time she went it was too late. The doctors said there were never going to be more babies."

"Then how…"

Nathan was fiddling with the cowboy hat he'd plucked off his head. His shirt was speckled from the rain, but his eyes were clear and steady. "We were both disappointed, but Mary was heartbroken. I blamed myself. She was barely nineteen. Hell, she was just a baby herself. I should have waited. I should have been able to control myself. But it was too late for that. We couldn't go back. I would have done anything to make her happy. We both wanted children. There was still one way to have them."

Crystal turned around as if to switch on another lamp. But really, she couldn't let him see her expression.

"We were living in Aberdeen," Nathan said, oblivious to the sudden patter of her heartbeat, the sudden knot in her stomach.

Aberdeen? The coincidences were mounting. Crystal needed to sit down.

"I was working for a mining company at the time," Nathan said. "So nobody here knows except my immediate family."

She skimmed a hand across the surface of an antique table. "Knows what?"

"We adopted Holly. We were never ashamed. God, it's the best thing we ever did. It's private, that's all. We told Holly, and my brothers know. It's nobody else's business."

Crystal's hand fell to the table with a thud just as lightning struck again. The room went dark and stayed that way.

"Damn. Where are your candles?"

She tried to pull herself together. Feeling her way to a shelf where several aromatic candles sat in a straight row, she struck a match to the first one, commending herself on how little her hand shook.

"You wanted to tell me something," he said from the other side of the room. "And I've done all the talking."

"We counselors tend to ask a lot of questions. It's one of the downfalls of the profession." Was that her voice, so natural sounding, so steady?

"In that case, Counselor, any suggestions for ways to talk Marsh into staying on a few more weeks?"

"Be honest." She took a shuddering breath and slowly turned to face Nathan. "If you want him to stay, tell him. Tell him why. And then accept his decision."

Nathan was in the process of putting on his hat when it occurred to him that there was something different about Crystal. He looked closely at her. The light of one candle simply wasn't enough to see her clearly. "I'm sorry, Crystal."

He'd surprised her. He'd have thought she would have been accustomed to his apologies by now.

"About what?"

"About hogging the center stage tonight. I have to go.

I'll talk to Marsh and then I'll come back so you can tell me what it was you wanted me to know.''

''No.''

''No?''

''It's getting late.''

She'd spoken fast. Too fast? ''Are you okay?'' he asked.

''Of course.''

''Then come here and kiss me.''

She walked directly to him, lifted her face and gave him a quick kiss.

''Not so fast.'' His arms went around her, his lips moving over hers. She started to soften, to warm, and he started to breathe easier.

But then the kiss ended. She backed out of his embrace a bit too quickly. In the instant it took her to pull herself together, Nathan saw something he'd never seen in her eyes. It was like a light that danced and flickered, nearly hidden beneath a bushel basket. She looked up at him, her eyes bravely holding his. Something unsaid passed between them.

Something intense flared through him. ''Invite me back.''

Her throat convulsed on a swallow. ''It really is getting late, Nathan. And Holly's due back tomorrow. And it's important to set a good example.''

He felt his eyes narrow. ''I hate to be the one to break this to you, but you just sounded suspiciously like Odelia Johnson.''

That brought out a small smile. ''Oh, dear. I really do need therapy.''

That was better, he thought. That sounded more like the Crystal he was coming to—

Thunder cracked again, making them both jump.

''Will I see you tomorrow?''

''If you want.''

There was something stilted about her answer, something

he didn't understand. "It's Ethan's turn to burn dinner. Would you like to sample it?"

Holly would be home by then, Crystal thought. Holly, who had been adopted by a couple living in Aberdeen about the same time Crystal was living in a town near there. Holly. Oh, Holly...

Crystal was having a difficult time behaving normally tonight. She knew she would never be able to pull off appearing nonchalant throughout an entire family dinner sitting across from the one girl in all the world who might be her—

"As delicious as that sounds, I think I'll pass," Crystal said. "It'll be Holly's first meal at home. And I have some things to do. Tell you what. I'll stop over after dinner."

"When?"

"When?"

"Yes. What time?"

"I'll surprise you."

Nathan didn't know what the hell was going on, but he knew he didn't like surprises. And he didn't like the pins and needles poking into the back of his neck. He kissed her once more, and then he walked out the door.

Crystal would never know how she found the strength to remain standing. The instant Nathan closed the door, she sank to the sofa like melting wax. A good analogy, all things considered.

She had to think.

She couldn't think.

At least not coherently.

She'd been in this town a year and a half. She'd seen Holly Quinn dozens of times. They'd laughed and talked. She'd given the girl a ride home. She'd sat a few feet away from her in her own car. And she hadn't so much as suspected. Why would she? She hadn't known Holly was adopted. They didn't really look alike. Holly's hair was darker, and straight. Her eyes were blue, not green.

Geoffrey's eyes had been blue.

Crystal jumped to her feet. She paced. She rammed her shin into a low table. And she paced some more.

Holly was fifteen and a half. Crystal remembered hearing that somewhere. At the time she hadn't thought anything of it. A lot of girls were fifteen and a half. Crystal's mind raced, her thoughts coming at breakneck speed. Nearly fifteen and a half years ago, Nathan and Mary Quinn had adopted a baby girl. Nearly fifteen and a half years ago, Crystal had given birth to one.

Was it possible it was the same child?

Yes, her mind screamed.

It was all so complicated. Oh, my God, she thought. She'd fallen in love with Holly's father. What was he going to say?

She didn't know what to do, what to tell him, what to say if she did tell him. If? She had to tell him. But first she needed proof.

"You should have seen the women out east!" Holly's voice was loud, exuberant. "Women you would never suspect would talk to a cowboy wanted to wear Uncle Zack's hat. Shoot, one lady tried to take off his belt."

"Holly, for crying out loud. Don't tell them everything!"

Nathan lifted one eyebrow shrewdly. "I want to know who was chaperoning who?"

Ethan turned to Crystal, who was sitting in an overstuffed chair. "Isn't that whom was chaperoning whom?"

The Quinn men had spent the morning unloading a truck of hay. They'd finished about the same time it started to drizzle again. Now they were all gathered in the living room. If anybody noticed that Crystal's smile seemed to be painted on today, they didn't comment, at least not to her, although she did catch Nathan watching her closely from time to time.

Holly screeched when Zack made a dive for her, giggling when she got away. Crystal's breath caught in her throat at the joyful sound. She had to work very hard to keep from staring. The girl brought so much life into this house. Zack made a second halfhearted attempt to grab Holly, and she made a second successful retreat, laughing all the while.

Crystal had never forgotten her baby's cry. But she'd never quite been able to imagine the sound of her child's laughter.

She wet her lips, swallowed the lump that rose to her throat. Nathan was looking at her again. Crystal reached for a teen magazine lying on the coffee table, feigning interest in belly button rings and fashion that fit in the palm of one hand.

"If I ever have kids, I'm only having boys," Zack said. "There's too much to worry about with girls. Every man out there is a potential hazard. Give me boys or give me nothing."

Holly piped up and said, "That sounds a little like give you liberty or give you death. What if your boys are like you?"

Zack blanched. Shoving his hair behind his ears, he said, "You're right. I wouldn't wish that on my worst enemy. That does it. No kids for me."

"I'd say that's a pretty safe bet," Marsh said, studying the cumbersome cast on his ankle. "Especially since there aren't enough women to go around in Jasper Gulch."

"Who would want you, anyway?" Ethan declared, giving Zack a brotherly shove. "Besides, Nathan's the one getting all the action around here."

Crystal, Nathan and Holly all froze. Nathan was the first to recover. "I'm not getting that much action."

"It's all right, Daddy. You're not getting any younger,

and I'm not going to be here forever. I'd feel better knowing you had somebody to take care of you.''

Ethan and Zack did a pretty good pantomime of a crotchety old man walking across the room. Straightening, they headed for different parts of the house. Marsh rose, too, spouting that since it looked as if he would be staying in Jasper Gulch a few more days, he had to make a phone call. He was still antsy, itching to get back to his work as a Texas ranger. He'd agreed to stick around for a few more days, to see Holly, and give his ankle a little more time to heal.

From the doorway Ethan told Nathan that he would start the dishes for him. Zack went to unpack. Holly hopped up, too, calling for second dibs on the telephone so she could call her best friend.

That left Nathan and Crystal alone in the room.

Striding to the chair where she was sitting, he said, ''It would only take a word from you and I could get out of washing dishes.''

''Far be it from me to upset the balance in the group dynamics of this family.''

Nathan shook his head. She was spouting psychiatric gibberish. Nothing unusual there. But she wasn't herself. ''You feeling okay, Crystal?''

More giggling rang out through the house as Marsh teased his niece. ''I feel a headache coming on.'' Crystal held up one hand. ''I know, I know. I'm usually the one who gives other people headaches.''

''Would you like some aspirin?''

''I have some in my purse.''

''A glass of water, then?''

''Nathan. I know where the kitchen is. If I didn't know you so well, I'd say you're stalling.''

He studied her through narrowed eyes. He could have sworn it made her nervous. In the end he said, ''I won't be long.''

Crystal had stopped in after dinner, and had ended up having dessert with all five Quinns. Alone in the living room, she had to remind herself to breathe. She hadn't lied. She really did feel a headache coming on. Rubbing at the knot at the back of her neck, she meandered around the room. Other than a big-screen television and some knick-knacks that were probably as old as she was, there wasn't a lot to look at.

The parlor beckoned, its doors open wide. She glanced all around. She told herself it was a good thing she had her psychology degree to fall back on, because she would make a terrible spy. Finding the coast clear, she wandered through the wide parlor doors. Just in case someone was looking, she didn't hurry directly to the piano where dozens of pictures stood in a layer of dust.

She went to the window first, and then to a low table, making the piano her last stop. She ran her fingers over the keys, then looked at the first photograph, a wedding picture in black-and-white. She assumed it was Nathan's parents. She thought the smiling, dark-haired baby in the next one was Nathan. Or maybe it was Marsh. Or Ethan. Or Zack. Shoot, they all looked alike.

"That's Daddy."

Crystal jumped.

"Sorry." Holly grinned. And Crystal tried to relax. It wasn't easy. Nothing was easy today. Certainly, it wasn't easy to keep from reaching a hand to Holly's hair.

"So you really have been spending time with my dad?"

Taking another deep breath, she said, "Some. He taught me to drive his motorcycle."

Holly smiled again, and Crystal melted a little inside.

"Uncle Ethan says you taught Daddy a thing or two, too."

Crystal thought Holly's sparkling personality must have been learned, not inherited. "It was all in good fun, Holly."

"Don't worry." She spun around, gliding to the window as if on colt legs.

Now there was a girl, Crystal thought, who could have been the dancer Crystal's mother had wanted. Of its own volition, her gaze went to a photograph of a round-faced baby with wisps of blond hair, a cherub's smile and only four teeth.

"That's me. Pretty ugly, huh?"

Crystal shook her head to clear it. Ugly? That was the most beautiful baby she'd ever seen. She knew, because she'd looked at the same child in another photograph nearly every day for the past fifteen and a half years.

There it was. Her proof. Her mind raced, her thoughts screamed. Oh, my God! It was true.

It was difficult to concentrate on everything Holly was saying. And Crystal didn't want to miss a word. Holly talked about how she was growing up, and how worried she'd been about her dad ever since her mom had died. Crystal noticed the way Holly moved around as she talked, as if she had more energy than she could contain.

Suddenly she returned to the piano. Pointing to a photograph, she said, "Wasn't she beautiful?"

Crystal stared at the picture of a petite, auburn-haired woman with sparkling brown eyes. She nodded.

"She lost her hair, but she never lost her spirit."

There was so much love and adoration in the girl's voice, so much exuberance in her smile, so much tenderness in her eyes. Crystal's throat closed up. She wondered how it would feel to be loved the way Mary had been loved.

Crystal refused to be jealous. Oh, but it wasn't easy. Mary was exactly the kind of mother she'd wanted for her child. The kind of mother she herself couldn't have been fifteen years ago. But now she could be. Not exactly like Mary, but a good, loving, living mother.

"You're the apple of your dad's eye. He said he's been proud of you since the day he and your mom adopted you."

"He told you that?"

What was it with the Quinns and their answers that were really questions? "It must be lonely for you, now that your mother is gone."

"I'm getting used to it."

"I had a friend in college who went looking for her birth mother when she was older."

Holly's face changed. Stubbornness settled in where a softer, gentler expression had been. "Why would I want to find someone who didn't love me enough to keep me?"

"But..."

"Not that I'm sorry she didn't. I had a mother, the best mother in the world. I don't want another. I have my dad and my uncles and my best friend."

Crystal fell apart inside, a little at a time.

The phone rang. Marsh yelled for Holly to get the extension in her room. Crystal had to get out of there before she fell apart completely. She went into the kitchen where Nathan and Ethan were doing dishes. Making excuses about her headache, she thanked Ethan for dinner, and told Nathan she really had to go lie down.

"I'll take you home."

"I drove over, remember? It's only a stone's throw away."

He walked her to her car. "I'll call you later."

She got in, started the engine and drove home. Once in her house, she took the stairs as if in a trance. She strode to her bedroom and sat on the edge of the bed. She stared at the photograph of her ba— of Holly.

Holly's words came back like taunts. "Why would I search for someone who didn't love me enough to keep me? I don't care. I don't want another mother...."

The first tear trailed down Crystal's face while she was trying to tell herself that Holly was simply going through a selfish phase. But Holly wasn't selfish. She was kind and energetic and sweet and smart and funny. It seemed she was more like the woman who'd raised her than the woman who had given birth to her.

Crystal had to face the dreadful fact that it was very likely Holly was never going to look for her birth mother. She didn't need another mother. She didn't love her birth mother. And she certainly didn't want her birth mother's love.

Crystal had moved to Jasper Gulch in case her daughter ever came looking for her. Holly was a quarter of a mile away. It might as well have been a thousand.

The second tear squeezed past her defenses. Falling back on the bed, Crystal fell apart the rest of the way.

The phone rang later that night. Nathan had said he would call. She knew if she didn't answer, he would come over. Sniffling, she picked it up. "Galloway residence."

"You sound terrible."

If every emotion hadn't been used up, she would have smiled. "Thanks, Nathan."

"You really are sick."

"There's something wrong with my sinuses."

"I'll be right there."

Crystal panicked. "No." She lowered her voice. "I was almost asleep."

"Oh. Well. Did you take something for it?"

"I think I just need a good night's rest." She needed about a hundred of them.

"But…all right. I'll call you tomorrow."

"Good night, Nathan."

She hung up the phone, thinking that tomorrow she was going to have to tell him who she was. She shuddered, because she was pretty sure she was about to lose him, too.

"You haven't lost Holly," she whispered to herself. "You can't lose something or someone you haven't had in fifteen and a half years."

Her mind, always rational and clear, knew it was true.

The tears started again. Switching off the light, she thought that maybe somebody should tell her heart.

A quarter mile away Nathan saw the light go off in Crystal's window. He sat in the dark on his bed, fully clothed except for his shoes and hat. Finally he hung up the phone on his end.

If she was almost asleep, why had she waited until now to turn out the light?

Something was wrong. What in blazes was going on?

Chapter Nine

Mondays were never good days. This particular Monday promised to be worse than most.

Dr. Kincaid saw patients until three on Mondays. It was necessary, because as he said, most people waited until holidays and weekends to get sick.

It was twenty after three when Crystal ushered the last patient of the day to the door. Isabell Masey talked all the while. Meredith had once proclaimed that Isabell was living proof that a leopard could indeed change its spots. Evidently, she'd been considered the town's biggest gossip for more than thirty years. These days the tall, thin woman, whose steel-gray hair matched her eyes, was happier and spoke of more positive things. Today Isabell clutched her purse in her bony hands, going on and on about how the Anderson "boys" were going to put Jasper Gulch on the map with their music.

Crystal nodded. Isabell talked.

Crystal smiled, and Isabell talked.

When Crystal yawned, Isabell said, "Late night, dear?"

"I didn't sleep well." She opened the door.

Isabell studied her closely. Once, she would have jumped to conclusions and left in a huff to tell one of her friends what she thought she knew. Today she said, "You do look a little pale, I'm afraid."

A little pale wasn't the half of it.

Crystal mumbled agreeably, and Isabell finally left. While straightening the desk and reception area, Crystal couldn't think of a better person to have scrutinized her appearance. Evidently, the cover-up stick she'd applied to the dark circles beneath her eyes had done the trick.

Grover and Pamela Sue Andrews had an appointment for another marriage counseling session at five. She considered going directly home to take a nap. Since she doubted she would be able to sleep, anyway, she decided to take a walk to try to clear her head.

The curtains didn't flutter in the house next door. Maybe things were looking up. She still didn't know what she was going to tell Nathan. She wished she could talk this out with someone, but there wasn't another soul she could tell. It had been years since she'd wished she had the kind of mother a grown daughter could turn to. She wished for it now.

Walking down Custer Street, she felt very alone. She turned right on Maple and ended up on Main Street. Cletus McCully was sitting on the bench in his usual spot in front of the post office. She spoke with him for a few minutes about the weather and the bottoming-out price of beef before continuing on up the street. The next thing she knew, she was opening the door at Hidden Treasures.

She told herself she only stopped by to see Meredith.

"Hi, Crystal!" Holly called, looking up from the antiques she was dusting.

Crystal melted inside. She was a lousy liar, even when she was lying to herself.

Holly was beautiful. Tall and lithe, she positively glowed. Her long, honey-blond hair swished like spun silk whenever she moved. Crystal felt as if she'd been dying of thirst for years. And suddenly, here was a fountain, bubbling before her eyes.

"Now I know why my dad didn't want me to go to Boston. You wouldn't believe how much homework I have to do tonight."

Holly talked as she worked. And Crystal really didn't see any reason to keep her distance. She'd spent most of the night trying to think of a way to tell Nathan that the daughter he was raising and the child she'd given up were one and the same. Along toward dawn an idea had crept into her mind: did she have to tell him anything?

Her conscience had been arguing with that thought all day. What harm could there be in keeping her secret a secret?

You love him. And it's very likely that he's falling in love with you. That isn't the kind of secret that is conducive to a loving, lasting relationship.

What did she know about loving, lasting relationships? It was something she'd craved all her life. That yearning for love and acceptance had led her down a path to heartache and a decision that had changed her forever.

Love. It wasn't easy, ever. It was harder for some than for others.

For her, it seemed to be destined to be a disaster.

Only if she told Nathan the truth. If she didn't, everything could stay the way it was. He could fall all the way in love with her, and she could go on loving him. Maybe she could never tell Holly that she was her birth mother, but she could be the girl's stepmother.

No. She couldn't do that. That kind of secret couldn't be kept from Nathan. Besides, what if Holly decided to search for her birth mother someday? What would she do if that search led back to her own doorstep?

Crystal always told the people she counseled to be honest with themselves and with each other. She knew she had to practice what she preached. She had to tell Nathan the truth, regardless of whether or not he told Holly, even if it meant she might lose him before she ever truly had him. In doing so, she might lose Holly, too.

"You're probably looking for Meredith, aren't you?" Holly asked.

"Oh, I don't know. I kind of enjoy talking to you."

Holly beamed, and Crystal had to work very hard to keep tears from springing to her eyes. Voices carried from the back room. The next thing Crystal knew, Meredith was hurrying toward her. Unfortunately, Harriet Andrews was close behind.

The room, all at once, was very quiet.

"Hi, Crystal!" Meredith was well aware of the dislike Harriet felt for Crystal. Heavens, Crystal thought. Harriet made sure everybody knew.

"I'll have Sky deliver your new sofa first thing tomorrow morning," Meredith said to Harriet. "Will someone be home at eight?"

Holly returned to her dusting, and since Meredith was busy with her customer, Crystal said goodbye and headed for the door. If she'd been looking, she would have noticed how quiet Harriet became, and how her eyes narrowed into slits as that inquiring mind of hers began adding two plus two.

Crystal never did get that nap. Nathan had called shortly after she returned home. He wanted to know how she was feeling. He told her he would see her later, his voice firm and final, as if daring her to make something of it.

"Later sounds nice," she'd said, meaning it.

Talking to him had relaxed her, leaving her hopeful. She prayed he would believe her when she told her she hadn't known that Holly was her daughter.

Why wouldn't he believe her? When had she ever lied to him?

Of course he would believe her. And after he cooled off, maybe he, a man who had dealt with his own feelings of guilt years ago, would understand.

Crystal studied her reflection in the mirror in the tiny powder room that was tucked beneath the stairs. She wouldn't win any beauty contests today, but splashing her face with cool water had brought a little color back into her cheeks. She was patting her face dry when she heard a car in the driveway.

She hung up the towel, switched out the light. Returning to the dining room, which served as her office, she eyed the antique clock on the mantel. Pamela Sue and Grover were early.

"Come on in, you two," she called when a knock sounded on the door. "You must really be dedicated to saving your marriage...."

The screen door creaked open. Already smiling, she turned at the first sound of footsteps.

Her smile drained away as she came face-to-face with Harriet Andrews.

Mondays. Crystal wanted to strike them all from the calendar.

"May I help you?"

"You most certainly may not!"

"Then what are you doing here?"

"I know your little secret, that's what."

Crystal refused to panic. "What secret is that?"

Harriet practically snorted. She was a short, squat woman with round hips and a large bosom. She should have looked soft. And yet the expression in her eyes was hard and flat, her face pinched. "I always thought there was something fishy about the way Nathan and Mary suddenly came back to Jasper Gulch with a baby. And Holly never did look like the Quinns or the MacDonalds. And then you moved here, and all this time you never dated any of the Jasper Gents."

Crystal's stomach lurched. Her throat went dry.

"What a coincidence that you waited until Mary had been gone a year to take up with Nathan."

"I care about Nathan, Harriet."

Harriet made a nasty sound through her pursed lips. "You remind me of Pamela Sue. You don't care about anybody except yourself."

Crystal had never wanted to hit anyone, and yet she had to fight the urge to slap that nasty face. "I'm expecting a couple any moment. If you'd like to make an appointment for later..."

Harriet's voice always carried. It rose to a fever pitch as she sputtered, "I didn't put it together until I saw you and Holly Quinn side by side this afternoon. The resemblance doesn't jump out at a person. It's carefully veiled, but it's there in the shape of your faces, your height, the way you move, sneaky as cats."

"Why are you telling me this, Harriet? Gossip like this usually keeps you on the phone for days."

Crystal knew she shouldn't be nasty at a time like this, but she couldn't help it. Harriet nearly shook with indignation. "I came to you because I want you to know that I'll be keeping your little secret."

Crystal did a double take.

Harriet's smile was as genuine as the alligator-skin purse she'd bought for six dollars at the five and dime a few years back. "On one condition."

Crystal swallowed nervously. "What condition?"

"You stop counseling my Grover and that, that woman, Pamela Sue."

The screen door was yanked open. "Oh, no you don't, Mother!"

"Grover!" Harriet exclaimed. "I didn't hear your car."

Grover warded off her touch. "I saw your car in the driveway and I was curious, so I parked down the road, and we walked up." Reaching behind him, he held the door for his wife. Once Pamela Sue was standing at his side, he said, "Your jealousy has gone too far, Mama. It's eating you up, and the part that's left, I don't even recognize. Now this is what you're going to do."

Harriet's mouth dropped open. "I don't care for that tone of voice, young man."

"I'm not a young man. I'm forty-one years old. You're going to put an end to this nastiness once and for all."

Grover wasn't a tall man. He wasn't even a muscular one. In some far corner of Crystal's overwrought mind, she acknowledged that he was a big man, just the same.

"You're going to be nice to Pamela Sue."

Harriet glared at Pamela Sue, making it clear that she would sooner be nice to a rattlesnake.

"I love her. And she loves me. And you're not going to breathe a word about Crystal's personal business."

"But..."

"Because I think that somewhere inside you, you're still the woman who raised me all by herself, the mother I love. And also, because you'll never see your first grandchild if you spill the beans."

"Grandchild!"

Pamela Sue, a voluptuous Southern belle, nodded, tried to smile, then burst into tears. Harriet's tears started immediately thereafter. Poor Grover was left taking turns patting their backs.

"I think it would be best if we rescheduled our appointment," he said.

"All right." Crystal sniffled, herself. Giving this family some privacy, she hurried out to the porch.

And almost ran headlong into Holly.

Holly froze.

Crystal reached a hand toward the girl. Holly jerked backward much the way Grover had a few moments ago. Crystal's heart cracked open.

Perhaps later there would be time to have the nervous breakdown she deserved. Right now she had to do what she could to take the hurt out of Holly's blue eyes and help her understand.

"I didn't know you were out here." When Holly didn't respond, Crystal said, "What are you doing here?"

Holly's horse nickered from the porch railing where it was tethered. "Daddy said you were sick last night. He wondered if you wanted to come over for supper. Is it true?"

There was no sense playing dumb, and Crystal wouldn't lie. She looked Holly in the eye, and in a very soft, quavering voice, said, "That you're my daughter? Ye—"

"Don't say that. Don't call me that. I'm not your daughter. And you're not my mother. Not the one who raised me. Not the one who counts. Not the one I loved."

The crack in Crystal's heart opened wider. "I didn't know, Holly. Until two days ago. I wasn't sure until yesterday, when I saw that picture of you as a baby. You're more beautiful than I could have imagined. I've always loved you...."

"You gave me away! My mother loved me. I can't believe Daddy would do this to me." She spun around, crying.

Crystal died a little inside. She wanted so desperately to touch Holly, and yet she couldn't. "Your father doesn't know. I'm going to tell him tonight. I'd like to be your friend."

Holly started down the steps. "Leave me alone." She flung the words out as she grabbed the reins and swung up onto her horse. "And leave my dad alone, too!"

"He has a right to know, Holly."

"Then everything would change, and everything's already changed too much." Crouching down, she urged the horse into a run. They scaled the stone wall, then disappeared on the other side of the mulberry bushes.

Crystal stood on her porch, the breeze cool on her tear-dampened face. She clutched her hands over her mouth to hold in the sob.

Monday. It couldn't get much worse.

Crystal made sure she was gone that entire evening. She'd caught a movie in Pierre, and although she'd had trouble following the plot, there had been plenty of ear-splitting sound effects to keep her from falling asleep. When the movie ended, she'd wandered into a grocery store that stayed open until midnight. She'd spent an hour buying two sacks of groceries she didn't need.

The light was flashing on the answering machine in the dining room slash meeting room when she returned. The first message was from Jayne Stryker, who was just calling to say hello. The second was from Nathan. She listened to it twice, just to hear his voice.

What was she going to do?

Holly didn't want her father to know. What could Crystal do?

For now, she carried the groceries into the kitchen and put them away. She hadn't eaten. So she cut into the three kinds of melons she'd purchased just so she could try out the new melon baller she'd had to have.

The phone rang before she'd polished off her bowl of perfectly shaped balls of fruit. She answered before the answering machine could click on. "Galloway residence."

"Didn't you get my message?"

"Nathan, we need to work on your hello skills."

"Why didn't you return my call?"

"It's midnight."

"I know what time it is, dammit. What's going on?"

She stretched the telephone cord as far as it would reach. She could see out the window. The mulberry bushes blocked her view of Nathan's house from the first floor.

"Where are you right now?" she asked.

"I'm in the study. Why?"

That meant he couldn't have seen her lights come on in the kitchen and dining room. He must have seen her headlights turn into her driveway.

He'd been watching for her.

"I thought you said you would see me tonight."

"Something came up."

She could picture him raking his fingers through his hair as he bit back a curse. "Crystal, stop talking like a counselor and tell me what's going on. Everybody's as jumpy as a cat on hot bricks. Even Holly's gotten in on it."

"Holly's edgy?"

"Edgy. The girl blew up tonight. She's like a damn volcano. Marsh, Ethan, Zack and I all tried, but nothing any of us said helped."

"Did she say what's wrong?"

"She said she wishes she'd stayed in Boston. I don't get it. I asked her if she missed the rehearsals, the museums and opera. For a second, when she rolled her eyes and told me nobody misses the opera, I glimpsed my girl. The next thing I knew she was throwing herself across her bed and sobbing that she misses her mom."

The clock blurred before Crystal's eyes. Officially, it wasn't Monday anymore. Tuesday wasn't promising to be any easier.

Bracing herself for what she had to do, Crystal said, "I think we should slow things down between us."

"I don't see what that has to do with—"

"I think she's upset about me. Maybe we should end it completely."

"Now wait just a minute."

"We could remain friends, of course."

"We're not going to remain friends, dammit."

"I'm sorry you feel that way, but I suppose that is your choice. Good night, Nathan."

"If you hang up on me, so help me, I'll be breaking your door down in two minutes flat."

If she could have, she would have smiled. Nathan Quinn may have been steadfast and strong, but he wasn't the most patient man on the planet, that was for sure. "All right. I haven't hung up."

"I'm coming over."

"Not tonight."

"When?"

She did what she could to disguise her shuddering breath. "I have time on Wednesday."

"You want to wait two days to talk about this?"

She decided not to mention that technically it was already Tuesday and, therefore, only one day until Wednesday. But no, she didn't want to wait until Wednesday. She wanted to talk about this right now.

She never wanted to talk about it.

"Yes," she answered. "It would be best to talk on Wednesday."

"Best for who? And if you say whom, I'll strangle you through the stinking phone wire."

"I'll see you Wednesday. Why don't you come here? About seven. Good night."

She hung up the phone as if it was hot. Inside, her blood ran cold. She'd finally found love. And in the process she'd discovered the daughter she'd always yearned for. And now, suddenly, both were slipping out of her reach.

She had to decide what to do, and she had to decide fast. Wednesday was right around the corner.

Nathan turned up the collar of his jean jacket against the unseasonable nip in the air. The sun was just beginning to dip toward the western sky. It was Tuesday. The Quinn brothers were mending fences. The literal ones. Ethan and Zack seemed to be enjoying the task. That probably had a lot to do with the stories about Boston Zack was undoubtedly blowing out of proportion. Not that good old Ethan cared.

It more than likely wasn't a coincidence that the younger two brothers had ended up working together. Nathan wouldn't have wanted to be around himself if he could help it, either.

Being around Marsh wasn't a lot better.

"I'm going back to the doctor tomorrow. If he won't take this stinking cast off, I'll take it off myself."

"Put a sock in it, would you?"

"Excuse me all to hell."

Nathan ran a hand over the stubble of a two-day beard. "Look. Wearing a cast like that must be annoying, uncomfortable and cumbersome as hell. But I've got bigger problems."

Marsh held the board in place while Nathan secured it with wire. "What kind of problems?"

"Women trouble."

"You mean Holly?" Marsh asked.

Nathan straightened, shrugged. "And Crystal."

"The old double whammy. I don't envy you. What's going on with those two?"

Nathan turned to stare at his most complex brother. Until that instant he hadn't considered the possibility that the two issues were related. Now that he thought about it, Holly had been fine until she rode over to Crystal's to invite her to supper last night. Crystal had been acting strange since Saturday.

"Something's going on," Nathan said. "Holly won't talk about it at all, and Crystal is putting me off until tomorrow night."

"Putting you off how?" Marsh hobbled to the stack of lumber for another board.

"That's when she says she'll talk to me."

"What's she waiting for?"

A few weeks ago Nathan would have answered with a cuss word. Tonight he shook his head and cast Marsh an imploring look.

Marsh planted his hands on his hips and said, "Okay, what are *you* waiting for?"

The brothers exchanged a long look. Nathan said, "I do believe that's the thousand-dollar question."

Marsh slanted Nathan a smile that had the power to make people on both sides of the law feel like his best friend one minute and his worst enemy the next. "Ethan! Zack! We're calling it a day. Unless you want to walk back to the house, let's go."

Ethan and Zack didn't have to be told twice. "Yee-ha!" Ethan said. "It's quittin' time."

Not for Nathan. He was just getting started. Something was wrong, terribly wrong, with Holly and with Crystal. Maybe it was related, maybe not. Regardless, he had to see Crystal.

Wednesday, ha!

Chapter Ten

Crystal leaned against the curved back of the old claw-foot bathtub and closed her eyes. Although the calendar indicated that it was nearing the end of May, there was a slight nip in the air tonight that should have made the long, hot bath feel luxurious. The bubbles she'd added to the water were dissipating, the only other sound that of the occasional water dripping from the faucet.

She'd read somewhere that a group of students majoring in English at UCLA were attempting to have the word *aquadextrous,* a word they deemed means possessing the ability to turn the bathtub faucet on and off with ones toes, added to the dictionary. There was a time when thinking about that sort of trivia had driven her nuts. Sliding her shoulders lower under the water, she figured it beat thinking about what she couldn't seem to stop thinking about these past four days.

Holly.

And Nathan.

And what Crystal was going to tell Nathan about Holly,

and whether she could tell him anything. And how could she not?

She opened her eyes at the sound of a car outside. She kept them open as she waited for it to drive by.

It slowed down. Why, it sounded as if it had pulled into her driveway.

She popped her head up, and peaked out the window. It was Nathan's truck. And it wasn't Wednesday.

She sat back down and listened intently. Seconds later a fist rattled her front door. She shivered from the chill in the air, but she didn't panic. The doors were all locked.

There was a slight crash. And then Nathan's voice called, "Crystal?"

He'd broken in!

Okay, now she was panicking. She pulled the plug and reached for her towel. Footsteps sounded on the stairs. "Nathan Quinn, you hold it right there!"

She was shoving her wet arms into the thin sleeves of her robe when she heard him say, "Sweetheart, now you're talking."

She just managed to get the front edges pulled together when he opened the door. His eyes glittered in the shadows in the hall. "Did I ever tell you I like bossy women?"

And here, all this time, she'd considered Zack the family rebel. Nathan's expression had bad boy written all over it.

"A decent man would turn around."

He hitched his hat higher on his forehead and leaned a shoulder against the doorjamb. So much for appealing to his sense of decency.

"You're early." She reached for her watch. "Twenty-three hours early." She had every right to sound huffy.

She was trying to think, and she couldn't think with him looking at her the way he was looking at her. She pulled the sash tight, knotted it twice.

He reached a hand to hers before she could tie it a third time. "Something's wrong," he said, his voice a gentle sigh, a slow sweep across her senses. "And I can't see what good it'll do to wait until tomorrow to fix it."

He drew her hand away from her sash and took her damp fingers in his. She'd missed him. It had only been two days, and she'd missed him. And he knew it.

She wondered if he was aware of the smile that stole across his face. She wondered if he was aware what that smile of his was doing to her. Her heart pounded an erratic rhythm. She cleared her throat, trying to begin.

He beat her to the draw. "Everything was fine until Saturday. I've been thinking about this for days, so don't try to deny it. You were going to tell me something after the dance. But you never did...."

"I've been trying to—"

"And it occurred to me that it wasn't fair to make you do all the talking."

"All the—"

He pushed himself away from the door and took a step closer. "You see, Crystal—"

"No, I don't see, and I don't know what you're—"

"I love you."

"You—"

"And you love me."

She didn't move, not even to breathe.

"You don't deny it, because it's true. I know it's happened fast. And I know some people are saying it's only a passing fancy. They're wrong. I've only loved two women in my entire life. When I find the real thing, I stop looking. I've found it with you."

Tears filled her eyes.

And he smiled. "I'm not usually a man of many words, so you'd better memorize these three words tonight. I love you."

Her heart fluttered, then rose all the way up to her throat. He reached a hand to her face. Lowering his head, he kissed her. The kiss sang through her veins, warming her from the inside out.

He loved her.

She'd waited all her life for somebody to love her. No, she'd waited all her life for *him* to love her. The crack in her heart eased together, and the knot in her stomach uncurled much the way the knots in her sash fell away beneath Nathan's hands. And then he was touching her, covering her breasts with his hands. Her hands were busy, too, pulling his shirt from his jeans and gliding around to the buttons, deftly slipping each from its opening.

It was the first time they'd ever been skin to skin, chest to breast, man to woman. He molded her to him, pressing her against him, fitting the curves and hollows of her body into the lines and planes of his. Still, they weren't close enough.

They ended up in her bedroom, where the last golden rays of the late-evening sun shimmered through her gauzy curtains. He reached for her hand, placing it over his heart. She could feel it beating there, galloping, for her.

He drew her toward the bed, and she went so willingly. He loved her. It sang through her mind, her heart, her soul. Nathan Quinn, Holly's father, loved her.

Everything inside her went perfectly still.

"Nathan."

His mouth ravaged hers. The man was in no mood to talk. She almost smiled. But she couldn't. Nor could she make love with him until he knew the truth.

"Nathan," she said again. "There's something I have to tell you. Something I've been trying to tell you for days, and I just haven't been able to, and then Holly came over, and she told me not to…"

She was rambling. That was Nathan's first coherent thought. His second was, she never rambled.

He drew far enough away from her to get a good look at her. Her face was pale, her green eyes hauntingly beautiful. Her ivory colored robe hung open, her breasts lush and white. She drew the robe together, and he forced his eyes away. His gaze flickered over a picture frame on the bedside table, his eyes focusing on the picture itself.

"Where did you get that picture of Holly?"

Silence.

He walked over to the table, studied the photo. He remembered the day it had been taken. Questions bombarded him, but until his blood made it back to his brain, he couldn't make sense of any of them. So he repeated the one he'd already asked. "Where did you get this picture of Holly?"

The floor creaked beneath her steps, her voice so quiet he had to concentrate to hear. "Mary sent it to me."

He turned to face her.

She held his eyes bravely. "Via Sherman Blair, of Smith, Dykstra, Livingston and Blair, Attorneys at Law."

The blood hit Nathan's brain like a tidal wave. His legs weren't fully operational, but all of a sudden his mind was. "What are you talking about?"

"I had a baby, Nathan."

"Yes. You and that professor. You lost her."

She shook in her effort to stay calm. "I didn't lose her. I gave her up. To a young married couple living in Aberdeen."

"You gave her up? For adoption?"

She nodded. "I didn't know the couple's names. But I chose them very carefully from the letters they wrote. From the letters you wrote. All I asked in return was a photograph of my baby. This arrived in the mail a year later." She bit her lip to keep it from quivering. "And then, a few years ago, I saw an article in a magazine. It was about a town in South Dakota that had advertised for women. The photograph was taken in the same diner where the baby's photograph had been taken."

"Then that's why you came here?"

"I didn't know, Nathan. I pray you can believe that. I didn't know Holly was the child I gave to an anonymous couple who wrote of a love of life and a commitment to family and to each other. I didn't know your name. But I think I loved you even then. And I loved Mary, too, like a sister I never had. Mostly, I loved my baby. And now Holly doesn't want anything to do with me."

Nathan sank to the bed. "Holly knows." No wonder she'd been acting so strange.

"She overheard Harriet Andrews spell it out on Monday."

"Wait a minute. Harriet knows?"

"Don't worry. She won't tell anyone. Grover made sure of that."

Nathan didn't know what Crystal was talking about. He'd never known Grover to stand up to his mother. That was the least of his worries. "It isn't as if I'm ashamed. Hell, Harriet can write it in the sky for all I care."

"Holly cares, Nathan."

He'd never heard Crystal's voice sound so small, so defeated, so sad. "How did you find her?"

"I didn't find her. I found you. I've been here for a year and a half. I'd heard that a couple who had an adopted daughter once lived in Jasper Gulch. I assumed it was my child, but then you started saying things that didn't make sense. The clues started mounting. And then I saw a picture of Holly in your parlor."

"Holly knows. She's upset," he said.

"Understandably so."

"It's been a hard year for her. A hard couple of years."

"You don't have to defend her to me, Nathan. I think that girl is pretty amazing. And although I didn't move here to find her, find her is what I did. I didn't move here to fall in love. And yet I did that, too. I certainly didn't move here to hurt Holly. I'm batting a thousand."

"I'll talk to her."

Crystal smiled, albeit sadly. "You can try. If she's anything like I was at her age, it won't do any good."

"What are you saying?"

She took an inordinate amount of time reknotting her robe. "I'm saying that Holly's the child here, the innocent one, the victim, if you will. Doing what was best for her fifteen and a half years ago was the hardest thing I ever did. Doing what's best for her now won't be any easier."

"You're talking as if this is over."

"It very well could be."

He strode to the doorway as if to leave. He backtracked at the last second. Reaching a hand to her shoulder, he turned her to face him and kissed her soundly on the mouth. "I'll talk to her."

He left then, and Crystal was left wondering if that might be the last time they ever kissed.

"What a week!" Ethan said.

"Yeah," Zack agreed.

"Would you pass me the corn, Holly?" Marsh asked.

Nathan finished dishing up his own plate. Marsh had done the cooking tonight. The barbecued spareribs were finger-licking good. Conversation, on the other hand, was stilted.

The weather had turned the corner from spring to summer. The wind almost always blew through this part of South Dakota. Today, it hadn't so much as fluttered the prairie grass growing tall on Quinn land. Nathan didn't mind the heat, but the silence in this house was damned unsettling.

He'd talked to Holly, and then he'd talked to Crystal. She'd been right. Holly wasn't taking the knowledge of her birth mother's identity well. It seemed to have brought the loss of her mother back in full focus. Strangely, or perhaps not so strangely, she'd wanted to talk about Mary. She wanted Nathan to relay every detail about how happy and loving and thrilled Mary had been the first time she'd held her baby when Holly was three days old. Nathan told her how Mary had sung her to sleep every night, and how she'd stayed up nights when Holly had been sick. He and Mary had explained how they'd come to be her parents when Holly was practically still in diapers. She'd grown up knowing it. She'd asked questions about her birth mother from time to time, and he and Mary had answered them as honestly as possible at the time. At the time it had seemed like a fairy tale. Now it was real.

Nathan believed the discovery would have been less traumatic for Holly if Mary were still here. But she wasn't. And it was up to him to make sure Holly understood that no one was going to hurt her. She'd tried to put on a happy face, but he knew she cried at night. And she'd stopped playing her violin.

He hadn't heard Crystal's music on the breeze in nearly a week, either. The only time she'd cried in front of him was the night she'd told him it would be best for everyone if they didn't see each other anymore. He'd wanted to argue, but in the end he'd thanked her for her sacrifice all those years ago, for it gave Mary, and him, the opportunity to be Holly's parents.

"Who wants more spareribs?" Zack asked.

Ethan shook his head. "So, Marsh, are you going to try to rent the Mulberry place out again before you go back to Texas?"

Every person sitting at the table jerked their heads around to stare at Ethan. It seemed only one of them could find his voice. "Why would I need to do that?" Marsh asked, reaching for a second helping of mashed potatoes.

"Crystal's moving out."

"She is?" Holly asked.

"Why?" Zack said.

"When?" Marsh said.

All three had spoken together. Nathan waited as long as he could to say, "Where is she going?"

Ethan held up both hands. "She's packing right now. I don't know where's she's going. Maybe somebody should ask her."

The remainder of the meal was eaten in silence. Marsh and Zack made noises about starting the dishes. Nathan knew it had to be pretty darn depressing in the dining room. Ethan had offered to help, too. He usually complained that he would sooner shovel out the horse barn than take his turn doing dishes.

Nathan and Holly were the only two remaining at the table. "So," Nathan said.

Holly didn't look up.

Nathan tried again. "The marching band is practicing after school every day next week for the Memorial Day parade. What time will you need a ride home?"

"You don't want her to move, do you?"

"Holly."

"I feel guilty, all right?"

Nathan pushed his coffee cup away from the edge of the table. Holly's face was narrow, her skin pale. Although he tried not to look for similarities to Crystal, every now and then he couldn't help but find one. Their likeness wasn't blatant. It was more like the subtle nuances in the music they both loved to play. Their faces were heart-shaped, their eyes clear, their lashes long and curled, their chins delicate.

"You have nothing to feel guilty about," he said. "You're hurting. And I feel God-awful helpless. I wish you were five again, or ten, so you could climb up on my lap and I could make everything better. I think your mom would know what to say. She was always better at these kinds of things than I am."

Holly raised her beautiful weepy blue eyes to his. "What do you think Mom would say?"

Nathan chose his words carefully. "I think she would

tell you that being adopted is nothing to be ashamed of. You're the best thing we ever did. Whose body you came from never mattered to us. And I don't care if you are fifteen, you're always going to be my little girl. But the fact is, without Crystal, I wouldn't have you.''

Holly sniffled. ''I don't want another mother!''

He didn't reply.

''I had the best mother in the world!'' She sprang to her feet and ran from the room.

Nathan heaved a sigh, thinking that she'd had the two best mothers in the world.

Chapter Eleven

The knock on her door was so faint Crystal didn't know how she'd heard it. She hurried to answer it, only to slow down at her first glimpse of Holly standing on her porch.

"I don't want another mom. I don't want you to think I do."

Crystal looked into Holly's eyes through the screen and nodded. "I understand."

In a voice gone noticeably softer Holly said, "Dad said you planned to keep me at first."

Again, Crystal nodded.

"What would you have named me?"

Biting her lip, Crystal absolutely positively forbade herself to cry now. "I'd narrowed it down to Portia or Prudence."

Holly pulled a face. "You're kidding."

And Crystal's grin came easier. "I know. Either name would have been totally wrong for you. What do you expect from a woman named Evangelina?" Her voice lowered in volume, but not in intensity as she said, "Giving you up was the hardest thing I've ever done. It was the rightest thing, too. Your mom did a fine job. I'm sorry I never knew her.''

Holly sniffled. ''I miss her. Dad does, too. But he loves you.''

Crystal practically floated the last few steps to the door. ''It doesn't mean he loved your mom any less. It doesn't even mean he doesn't still love her.''

''I know. But Uncle Ethan said he acted different with you. He even *sounded* different every night when I called from Boston. It was like he was young or something. It's embarrassing.''

Crystal gave up and let the tears trail down her cheeks, unchecked.

When Holly sniffled, Crystal reached for the box of tissues. Keeping one for herself, she pushed the door open several inches, and offered one to Holly. The girl took it, box and all. ''I was thinking,'' she mumbled, ''that maybe you shouldn't leave.''

Beyond Holly, Crystal saw Nathan step out of the gap in the mulberry bushes. Her gaze returned to the girl struggling with her next words.

''My mom will always be my mother.''

''I'd like to learn more about her, Holly.''

''You would?''

''Yeah. And if you'd like, I'll show you the essay she wrote about how she felt about becoming a mother. Your mother. You can read your dad's, too. He might be a man of few words, but when it's absolutely necessary, he can be very eloquent. I believe he says what he means and means what he says.''

''Tell me about it!''

Crystal prayed it was only one of many moments of shared camaraderie. But she didn't dare say it out loud.

''Then you'll stay?'' Holly and Nathan had spoken at the same time. Father and daughter shared a small shrug and a heartfelt sigh.

"I'll stay," Crystal said, plucking a tissue from the box now in Holly's hands.

She wanted so badly to wrap her arms around Holly and hold her the way she had when Holly had weighed seven and a half pounds. It was too soon. Perhaps one day...

Holly, seemingly ill at ease, took a backward step. "You two probably have stuff to talk about."

"Do you have any pointers for me, Holly?"

The girl cast Crystal an expression only a teenager could pull off. "You're the counselor!"

Crystal shrugged. "Knowing what to say to people I truly love is different from telling other people how to communicate with each other."

With a shake of her head Holly smiled shyly at Crystal and spoke to Nathan on her way by. Nathan waited to look at Crystal again until after Holly had mounted her horse and ridden away.

"What did Holly say?" she asked.

He swept his hat off his head. "She told me not to do anything she wouldn't do."

As he strode closer, the intensity in his eyes reached inside Crystal, spreading to a place beyond her heart, a place she couldn't name. She felt a curious sense of déjà vu, as if she was coming home. Which was strange, because he was the one moving closer.

"That's quite a girl you have there," she said.

"I have you to thank for that. I have you to thank for a lot of things."

There were a dozen reasons, all of them good, why Crystal should have let it go at that. There was only one reason that she didn't. She loved him, and she wanted to hear what was in his heart. "Like what?"

"Oh," he said, "let's see. I have you to thank for hanging your shingle in Jasper Gulch. Pamela Sue and Grover are working out their problems because of you. Much to Harriet's annoyance. The eleventh- and twelfth-grade girls know how to defend themselves, thanks to you. Much to the annoyance of the eleventh- and twelfth-grade boys. Generally, people who talk to you learn how to talk to each other. Even Marsh and I are getting along better these days.''

''You don't say.''

''You can be a bully and a brat. Which is exactly what it's going to take to keep the likes of me in line.''

Soft thoughts shaped her smile. ''You make it sound so appealing.''

Nothing about the conversation should have been lust arousing, and yet Nathan's desire for this woman had never been stronger. The closer he came to knowing her, the more certain he was that he wanted to make her his.

''You'll stay, won't you, Evangelina?''

She met him at the bottom of the steps, her face lifting as his lowered. Their kiss was just a brush of air at first, slowly growing more intimate, enhanced by her gentle sway toward him and his slight tilt and turn, until their lips were fully joined. It brought more than a rush of blood and flutter of hearts. It brought a sense of burgeoning joy and peace, as if in this kiss, secrets were held safely, and they were both home.

''Is that a yes?'' he asked.

''On one condition.''

''Oh. We're naming conditions now are we?''

''I am. You're not.''

He chuckled. ''What condition?''

''Don't ever call me Evangelina again.''

''I can't promise you that.''

For an instant the old Crystal reared her head. ''Why the heck not?'' she asked.

''Because I think it's only fair that our children know their mother's full name.''

''Our children?''

He nodded. ''We're young enough to have them. Hell,

according to Holly, Ethan and Marsh, I was acting sixteen a few weeks ago. Holly's always been enough for me, and if you don't want more, I'll understand...."

She reached a hand to his face, placing a finger on his mouth to silence him. "Um, Nathan? Aren't you getting the cart ahead of the horse, here?"

"You don't want more children?"

"There's nothing I want more than to build a life with you, and Holly, and to have another child or two."

"Or three."

"Or three? We're going to have to talk."

He drew her finger into his mouth and nipped it.

"Why you..."

He swooped down as if to cover her mouth with his. She turned her head at the last second. "Not so fast, cowboy."

Strains of violin music carried on the evening breeze. "I recognize that song," Crystal whispered. "It's a love ballad."

"Holly's serenading us."

She looked at him, hesitantly and then expectantly. Suddenly Nathan understood what Crystal was waiting for.

He moved his hat to his left hand. Going down on one knee, he reached for her right hand. His proposal to Mary had been something to the affect of "Oh, my God, are you sure? Then we'll get married. Yeah, that's what we'll do." He was older now, and his love for Crystal was different. It went every bit as deep, but the years had added a dimension to his life and a knowledge that couldn't help but make him a better, deeper, more caring man. Crystal had been through so much, had given up so much. She deserved everything he had to offer and then some.

Still on one knee, he looked up at her. "Will you marry me, Crystal?"

A tear trailed down her cheek. She swiped it away with one hand. "Just try to stop me."

The last thing Nathan had expected to do was laugh. He

never knew what she was going to say. That alone promised to make the future interesting. But there was so much more in his future.

He sprang to his feet and kissed her. Her mouth opened beneath his in a kiss full of need, a kiss full of giving and taking, of passion and excitement.

Sometime later he took her hand again. Together they strolled up the porch steps, then sat close together on Hester's old porch swing. He wrapped his arm around her shoulder, and she set the swing in motion.

The branches of the mulberry bushes sang in the evening twilight. Hearts full, Crystal and Nathan listened to the beautiful, poignant strains of their daughter's violin.

"Are you asleep?" he whispered when the song ended.

"No. I was just thinking."

"About what?"

"About life and fate and how everything feels so right. And how Harriet and Odelia were wrong. I wasn't a passing fancy, after all."

"You're a spring fancy, that's turning into the rest of our lives."

"I was thinking that we should thank Marsh for renting this place to me, too. Which brings me to one more thing. I would love to have children with you. And don't you think it would be fitting to name our first girl after the entity that brought us together?"

"You mean Marsha?"

"No."

"Tell me you aren't thinking of naming a child Hester."

She elbowed him. "I would like to name a girl Spring."

"And if we have a boy?"

"Pierpont."

The swing jerked to a stop. He was shaking his head even as his hands went to her shoulders. "Crystal!"

"Communication," she said, "is the key to a successful relationship."

He placed his hand over her mouth first. Bending closer by inches, he said, "I have another form of communication in mind."

"Oh," she said, when his mouth covered hers.

And, much later, "Oh, my."

His form of communication hadn't been covered in psych class. Perhaps that was because that kind of communication would have made the need for counselors obsolete.

"Is there anything you want to add?" Nathan asked sometime later.

She reached up and rested her forehead against his. "There is one thing I would like to hear you put into actual words again."

His eyes darkened, his pupils so big only a circle of brown surrounded them. "I love you, E. Crystal Galloway."

"And I love you."

Her eyes closed, her heart brimming with so much love and happiness she couldn't contain it all. It spilled over into Nathan's heart. And then, as though it had arms, their love covered them both like a warm breeze and a gentle sigh.

* * * * *

In July 2001

New York Times bestselling author

DEBBIE MACOMBER

joins

DIANA PALMER

&

Patricia Knoll

in

TAKE5

Volume I

These five tender love stories
are quick reads, great escapes
and deliver five times the love.

Plus

With $5.00 worth of coupons inside,
this is one *sweet* deal!

HARLEQUIN®

Makes any time special ®

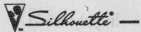

Don't miss the reprisal of Silhouette Romance's popular miniseries

When King Michael of Edenbourg goes missing,

Royally Wed
The Stanbury Crown

his devoted family and loyal subjects make it their mission to bring him home safely!

Their search begins March 2001 and continues through June 2001.

On sale March 2001: **THE EXPECTANT PRINCESS**
by bestselling author **Stella Bagwell** (SR #1504)

On sale April 2001: **THE BLACKSHEEP PRINCE'S BRIDE**
by rising star **Martha Shields** (SR #1510)

On sale May 2001: **CODE NAME: PRINCE**
by popular author **Valerie Parv** (SR #1516)

On sale June 2001: **AN OFFICER AND A PRINCESS**
by award-winning author **Carla Cassidy** (SR #1522)

Available at your favorite retail outlet.

Silhouette®
Where love comes alive™

Meet 50 loving dads in

babies & BACHELORS USA

Take 4 FREE BOOKS,
Plus get a FREE GIFT!

Babies & Bachelors USA is a heartwarming new collection of reissued novels featuring 50 sexy heroes from every state who experience the ups and downs of fatherhood and find time for love all the same. All of the books, hand-picked by our editors, are outstanding romances by some of the world's bestselling authors, including Stella Bagwell, Kristine Rolofson, Judith Arnold and Marie Ferrarella!

Don't delay, order today! Call customer service at
1-800-873-8635.
Or
Clip this page and mail to The Reader Service:

In U.S.A.
P.O. Box 9049
Buffalo, NY
14269-9049

In CANADA
P.O. Box 616
Fort Erie, Ontario
L2A 5X3

YES! Please send me four FREE BOOKS and FREE GIFT along with the next four novels on a 14-day free home preview. If I like the books and decide to keep them, I'll pay just $15.96* U.S. or $18.00* CAN., and there's no charge for shipping and handling. Otherwise, I'll keep the 4 FREE BOOKS and FREE GIFT and return the rest. If I decide to continue, I'll receive six books each month—two of which are always free—until I've received the entire collection. In other words, if I collect all 50 volumes, I will have paid for 32 and received 18 absolutely free!

267 HCK 4537
467 HCK 4538

Name	(Please Print)		
Address			Apt. #
City		State/Prov.	Zip/Postal Code

* Terms and prices subject to change without notice.
Sales Tax applicable in N.Y. Canadian residents will be charged applicable provincial taxes and GST. All orders are subject to approval.
DIRBAB02   © 2000 Harlequin Enterprises Limited

SILHOUETTE®
MAKES YOU
A STAR!

Look in the back pages of
all June Silhouette series books to find an
exciting new contest with fabulous prizes!
Available exclusively through Silhouette.

Don't miss it!

Silhouette®
Where love comes alive™

P.S. Watch for details on how you can meet
your favorite Silhouette author.

COMING NEXT MONTH

#1522 AN OFFICER AND A PRINCESS—Carla Cassidy
Royally Wed: The Stanburys

Military law forbade their relationship, but couldn't stop the feelings Adam Sinclair and Princess Isabel Stanbury secretly harbored. Could they rescue the king, uncover the conspirators—*and* find the happily-ever-after they yearned for?

#1523 HER TYCOON BOSS—Karen Rose Smith
25th Book

Mac Nightwalker was wary of gold-digging women, but struggling single mom Dina Corcoran's money woes touched the cynical tycoon. He offered her a housekeeping job, and Dina quickly turned Mac's house into the home he'd never had. Did the brooding bachelor dare let his Cinderella slip away?

#1524 A CHILD FOR CADE—Patricia Thayer
The Texas Brotherhood

Years earlier, Abby Garson had followed her father's wishes and married another, although her heart belonged to Cade Randell. Now Cade was back in Texas. But Abby had been keeping a *big* secret about the little boy Cade was becoming very attached to....

#1525 THE BABY SEASON—Alice Sharpe
An Older Man

Babies, babies everywhere! A population explosion at Jack Wheeler's ranch didn't thrill producer Roxanne Salyer—she didn't think she was mommy material. But Jack's little girl didn't find anything lacking in Roxanne's charms, and neither did the divorced doctor daddy....

#1526 BLIND-DATE BRIDE—Myrna Mackenzie

Tired of fielding the prospective husbands her matchmaking brothers tossed her way, Lilah Austin asked Tyler Westlake to be her pretend beau. Then Tyler realized that he didn't want anyone to claim Lilah but him! What was a determined bachelor to do...?

#1527 THE LITTLEST WRANGLER—Belinda Barnes

They'd shared a night of passion—and a son James Scott knew nothing about. Until Kelly Matthews showed up with a toddler—the spitting image of his daddy! When the time came for Kelly to return to college, could James convince her he wanted both of them to stay...forever?

RSCNM0501